BAD
CONNECTIONS

Books by Joyce Johnson

Bad Connections

Come and Join the Dance
(by Joyce Glassman)

BAD CONNECTIONS

by
Joyce Johnson

G. P. Putnam's Sons
New York

SBN: 399–12122–6

Library of Congress Cataloging in Publication Data

Johnson, Joyce.
   Bad connections.

   I. Title.
PZ4.J69177Bad   [PS3560.03795]   813'.5'4   77-16367

Portions of this book have previously appeared in *Ms.* Magazine.

For Berenice Hoffman

There is a certain intensity in endings. Where passion has run dry, where hot has become cold, where love is no longer distinct from habit, disguising simple fear of the unknown, where there has been for some time a nullity—there may be in the last attempts at salvage a raising of certain questions previously seemingly forbidden, the covering stripped off mysteries upon which the original contract rested. For an imperfect bond between two people is often based upon a tacit ignorance. There is more compromise than choice in most relationships.

Appearances to the contrary, I've learned I am not a compromiser. For too many years I dreamed my life and then I decided to wake up. A certain violence in my methods, a single-mindedness of focus, came as a shock to others. One man, well known on the left, once angrily called me a guerrilla. Another lover, if I can accurately call him that, accused me of wanting, wanting too much.

And indeed I wanted everything, much more than he ever imagined, much more than I would have dared to say—since there is a fearful fragility in men that always makes it impossible for me to be explicit with them. And then there was my own fragility as well—a thin membrane sagging under the weight of longings.

The year I turned thirty-five a hunger flared. The lights of the so-called real world dimmed, and in the hot glare of my imaginings, I found myself alive in the most fevered colors—there and in the reflections I caught for moments in the eyes of others.

I was married once to a man who is still an enigma to me. I do not know to this day precisely why I married him or precisely who he is. He was a man who seemed to lack any history. He might have been born the day I met him. He made a very good first impression—tall and handsome in a careless, shambly way. And there was a boyishness about him then that appealed to me, a kind of ingenuousness and optimism. He liked to dance, although there was something clumsy and mechanical about his style, and we went to a lot of loft parties and East Village discotheques and spent a lot of time in bed. I married my dancing partner. I remember the throbbing music of those late nights, the whirling, spangled globe on the ceiling of the Electric Circus gilding the upturned faces of the dancers. He moved in with me and I got careless with my diaphragm and became pregnant. He married me even though he was categorically opposed to marriage and didn't want children. I promised him nothing would change. It was not a good bargain.

I have mentioned his lack of history. I accepted not only that but his lack of a present. For six years we inhabited the same space, exchanged certain services—or rather *I* exchanged certain services. I see this gray blur of a woman leaving her office, hurrying downtown at the end of the day to pick up the baby from the sitter, stuffing groceries and laundry into the stroller with the sense that her identity is leaving her, that she is going home to nothing. And yet she must go home. Where else would she go? She is cooking dinner to the drone of the television which is always on when she is there and he is asking her to tell the baby to be quiet because between the water rushing into the sink and the noise the baby is making, he cannot hear the seven o'clock news and it is very annoying. "Tell the baby to be quiet yourself," she says. And later when he has gone out to the bar or discotheque—from which he will return at five, six, seven in the morning, although all such places by state law close at four—she turns off the television set and every light in the house and crawls into bed and waits to become unconscious.

They are about to have a conversation which later she will recognize as terminal. They are lying in bed, having made it for the first time in several weeks. The child has been sent away to the country. The house is very quiet without the child, who even when sleeping is a presence that can be felt. He blames the child sometimes for their sexual difficulties. Hasn't she noticed how the child has a way of waking out of the deepest sleep, of calling out for her just at the crucial moment? It is as if the little guy has a perverse sixth sense, a radar that tells him when his parents are going to fuck and sets him off like an alarm. The logical solution then, she thinks—the Malthusian solution—would be to get rid of the little guy and all would then be well. She waits for him to make this suggestion.

Tonight without the child here he was deliberately experimental, directing her in attempting different positions, turning her from one side to the other with varying placements of knees, his orders brusque and impatient. She had the feeling he was methodically following some invisible text. She was clumsy and stiff—not at all, she supposes, like the limber girls of the bars, with their yoga and tai chi classes, their expertise in the fifty erotic positions, their yin and their yang. Tonight he is very angry with her because her legs are too short. That is the reason they have been having such difficulties. He is convinced now that their bodies just don't fit each other. A cruel trick of fate for him to have ended up with such a short-legged woman!

She can remember a time in the past when they fitted each other perfectly, but doesn't bother to say it. She is comforting herself, warming herself, with thoughts of Conrad her lover, who is not as long-limbed as Fred her husband but bulkier. She would like to be lying against Conrad's huge chest and belly, her face buried in his mat of red hair.

Still, she feels she should explore with this boylike man she has lived with the real nature of their difficulties. There is still time for understanding, and understanding is something she believes in very strongly. She would like to understand more and feel less. She would like to be omniscient and thus distant. She is most of all simply curious about this person—she has lived for years with him in a state of suspended curiosity. Who is he? she wonders now for almost the last time, looking at the remote face that is becoming somewhat jowly.

11

She opens the conversation in an oblique way that is characteristic of her style—leading off with a tangential question, rather than getting right to the point.

"You've never told me much," she says, "about your relationships with other women. I know you've had relationships before me. You've never said what they were like."

"Why are you asking now?" he says suspiciously.

"Because I think it's one of our problems that you never talk about youself. I think it's weird, for example, that I don't know anything about these other relationships."

"You think it would help if we talked about these things."

"I don't know that it would help, but it might. Maybe nothing will help," she says. She is speaking very collectedly, with an almost disinterested tone. She waits. He is silent. "I thought I would ask, that's all," she says.

There is an odd smile on his face. Perhaps he is taking a journey into the past. "There was an Argentinian girl I knew in Paris—" he begins.

"Yes?" she says.

"Well, she had the most fantastic muscles in her vagina. She could do the most incredible things. It was an extraordinary experience. And there was another girl I lived with for a few months. Arlene. She was from a Polish family."

"You lived with her?" the interviewer probes.

"Yes. It was a disaster. I think I stayed with her chiefly because she knew how to suck my dick and that's what we did most of the time."

"And what about me?" she asks.

"What do you mean, what about you?"

"What about me? What's my specialty aside from being Jewish?" She sits up in bed now and stares at him. She wants to be very sure of his answer.

12

"What are you talking about?" he says disapprovingly.

"I want to know about me! What's my specialty? What's my specialty?" she cries, digging her fingers into his shoulders and shaking him. "What's my specialty?"

He is looking at her with amazement. "There's nothing special about you."

It is six o' clock in the morning and she has just left her husband. She is walking on her short legs to the West Side IRT subway, noticing how the light hits the buildings at this unusual hour, so that they look very starkly outlined and opaque. There is something very definite about the shadows they cast. She is aware of herself noticing things. She is walking very swiftly with the long strides that a taller person might make, her arms swinging freely. She was in such a hurry to get out before he woke that she forgot her purse. But she will not go back for it. There is a dollar in her pocket, more than enough to get her uptown to Conrad.

Her mind is very keen and clear. It has not been this clear in years. If she had nothing to go toward, she knows she would be in pain. But she is lucky, a very lucky woman to have met Conrad at this juncture in her life, to have been chosen by him from all the other pebbles on the beach. She'd thought she was becoming invisible, but he saw her just in time. She will tell him about the conversation she had with Fred, how she asked him to name her specialty, and he will laugh with her at the awfulness of it—because she knows it is not only awful but funny—and hold her against him and lead her gently back into the bedroom and put his hands under her shirt upon her breasts, squeezing them until she gasps and moans, his blue eyes resting seriously, ardently, upon her.

She waits impatiently for the subway. It comes at last and grinds from station to station. She wishes now she

13

had brushed her teeth. She wishes herself already at his door. She gets out at 79th Street and speeds along the two blocks to his house. Six-thirty now. She flashes by a disheveled image of herself in the rear view mirror of a car. She wonders if she should have called him. It's not like her to turn up anywhere without an appointment. But this is different. It is an emergency. The beginning of the future. Just before she goes into Conrad's building, she looks up at his windows on the second floor, where grimy venetian blinds have been drawn down to the sills. She tries to see if there is a light on, but of course there is none. Of course he is still asleep.

The night doorman comes toward her as she pushes open the heavy glass door and steps into the lobby.

"Schwartzberg," she says firmly.

"Two J," he says, staring at her curiously.

She feels the need to declare herself legitimate. "I'm expected," she says and presses the button for the elevator.

She gets off at the second floor and walks down the corridor. It is perfectly still. No one is up in any of the apartments. There is not even the sound of a child's cry or a radio. Copies of the *New York Times* lie folded and unread on doormats. She thinks that she and Conrad will have breakfast together this morning for the very first time. Perhaps she will make coffee for him while he looks at the paper. How extraordinary that they will do anything as ordinary as that.

She rings his doorbell once lightly, then waits and rings again, pressing harder now. She can hear the buzzing inside his apartment. She can see the apartment in her mind's eye—the piles of books, the ash-filled coffee cups, all undisturbed since her last visit. Perhaps he is in a very deep sleep. She feels guilty now for having to

14

wake him. He has told her how hard he's been working, how exhausted he feels. There are too many demands on him, he says. But this is not a demand. She is bringing him herself. She presses again, keeping her finger on the bell for a much longer time. "Conrad!" she calls, putting her mouth close to the door. "Conrad!"

She looks down at her feet at the folded *New York Times*. There is another folded newspaper under it. It is yesterday's. And under that there is mail, yesterday's mail, because today's could not have been delivered yet. There is a phone bill, a copy of the *National Guardian*, an overdue notice from the library, and a letter in a blue envelope from a woman named Betty Klein in Berkeley. She holds all this mail in her hands, reading the name Conrad Schwartzberg over and over again. She wonders if this can really be happening to her, if she has really come up here at this hour to stand outside Conrad Schwartzberg's door holding these pieces of paper, if all this can possibly indicate what it seems to indicate.

After a while, she goes away, first putting the mail back where she had found it, the two newspapers neatly on top of it, first yesterday's, then today's. It is all in perfect order. As she steps into the elevator, she realizes she has left no traces.

My relationship with Conrad Schwartzberg was characterized by bad connections—missed appointments, late trains, automotive breakdowns, fogged-in airports, abruptly cut-off phone conversations. I learned early that I would not find Conrad where I thought him to be. I got used to it in the end, got used to it to some extent. No, never really got used to it. He was a man who moved constantly, who could drop out of reach for days or weeks—to reappear without apology. I collected his various phone numbers, even the ones I wasn't supposed to have. These testified to my developing Nancy Drew-like capabilities, my occasional triumph in being one jump ahead of him. I held them in reserve in case I needed them. More and more I became a woman who lived by her wits.

And yet all that tireless motion that Conrad embodied drew me to him, held me enchanted. I wanted only to move with him. I waited for him to invite me to abandon my predictable and sedentary existence—nearly as predictable and sedentary after I left my husband as before, except for the turmoil Conrad had added to it.

There was a blues that was popular for a while in the late fifties, when I came of age. I remember the lyrics to this day with a combination of nostalgia and fury:

> Goin to Chicago, baby
> Sorry I can't take you.
> Ain't nothin in Chicago
> That a monkey woman can do.

At thirty-five I was still a romantic, still waiting for an opportunity to go "on the road," at least figuratively.

Once Conrad took me to Buffalo. Another time we almost went to Cincinnati for the weekend—except his mother went into a severe depression at the last minute, or that's what he said. Twice—both times disastrous—I followed him to California. Still, I owe to Conrad a brief trip across the border into Mexico, as well as my first night—believe it or not—in what he assured me was a prototypical motel, which was even located off a freeway a few miles outside L.A. It had a swimming pool we didn't swim in, a big color TV with special pornographic movies that we didn't watch, a paper bathmat that read YOUR PERSONAL BATHMAT, and drinking glasses shrink-packed in plastic. We put down our suitcases and made love on the color-coordinated bedspread for the third-to-last time.

He had a little green Saab when I first knew him, a ridiculously small vehicle for a person of his proportions. He filled almost the whole front seat with his bulk, his belly wedged up against the steering wheel. The Saab was as dusty as his apartment and it was filled with the apartment's overflow of Marxist studies and law journals, stacks of undelivered leaflets that were months obsolete, and discarded articles of clothing. It was my joy to occasionally ride in it with him—to a speaking engagement in Larchmont, a rally in New Paltz, a fundraising dinner in Hempstead. He was at the height of his career as a radical lawyer, having taken on the defense of the Mahwah Seven, and he was much in demand on the Left as a speaker at meetings of all kinds. I would sit unobtrusively in the audience and listen to him proudly—tears would roll down my cheeks when he'd invoke the vision of a "new society." He had a way of pacing the platform, as if even there he could not be contained in his assigned place behind the podium.

Conrad. He was named that by his working-class father, a fur-cutter who had a lifelong appreciation of the classics. Do names shape personalities? Would Conrad have been different if he had been named Edgar after Poe, another of his father's favorites, or something as prosaic as Howard after no one in particular? Like the famous author of *The Heart of Darkness* and *The Secret Agent*, he has been a restless wanderer as well as a self-made intellectual. About both men there is something mysterious, the sense of a hidden life. And my Conrad too, an enthusiastic starter of so many things, has been prolific in his way. Leaving the personal out of it, I refer to defense groups, collectives, journals, movements and even some writings—not any of which match the fervor of his verbal style. Perhaps at this very moment Conrad is sitting in a meeting of some committee he has just organized, waiting his turn to speak. His head is down, he crouches like a prizefighter waiting to come out of his corner. Characteristically, he is running both of his hands through his hair, that red cherubic tangled curling mass that was once my delight. In a moment he will stand up and turn the whole thing around.

19

❀ ❀ ❀

She is in her office but her mind is still reeling through the city, in transit between Sheridan Square and the Upper West Side. She calls Fred and tells him she had felt the urge to take an early morning walk. She borrows ten dollars from petty cash and goes downstairs to the drugstore in the lobby. She buys a comb, a toothbrush, a pinker lipstick than she usually wears and some green eyeshadow, and puts the change in the small paper bag these articles come in.

Back at her desk she selects a sharpened pencil and hangs on to it, staring at a paragraph on the proof sheet in front of her. She knows already that it is not going to be a good day for concentration. She is staring at the opening of an essay by an eminent cultural critic:

There is no doubt that we have ex perienced in our own lifetimes, even in those rare in stances where we are in sulateed somewhat

She does not catch the typo in the spelling of *insulated*, which will annoy the eminent critic considerably, when he finds *insulateed* right in the first sentence of his essay on illiteracy in the fall issue of *New Thought*. She is imagining Conrad walking into his office on West Twenty-first Street any minute now—Conrad back from wherever he has been, rumpled and unshaven, wearing the same clothes he had on yesterday when he called her and said nothing about being out of town.

against the shock s of the onslaught, the profound and inescapably de leterious effects of mass-

At her right elbow there is the telephone. She feels

20

slightly nauseated. She knows she is going to end by dialing the number of Conrad's office. She asks herself not to, but she does.

A young woman, an ex-girlfriend of Conrad's who is now a part-time secretary at the People's Law Collective and is working her way through law school, answers. She says that Conrad isn't in. "We don't expect Conrad until later this afternoon. Any message?"

She almost says, "Tell him Molly called," but doesn't. This way if she doesn't reach him it will be by default as if she hadn't called him in the first place.

She hesitates for a moment or two, then calls Conrad at home. The line is busy. She sees a door with nothing in front of it. One copy of the *New York Times* is in the garbage. The other is spread out in front of Conrad on the kitchen table next to the opened mail.

She calls back a few minutes later. This time there is no one there.

"Hello," Conrad said to me. "How are you?"

Since I hadn't considered the possibility that Conrad might call me before I reached him, I was so thrown off guard I nearly said I was fine.

"Not so good."

"Oh? That's too bad." There was the usual good-natured warmth in his voice. "Did something happen?"

"Conrad, I was at your house at six-thirty this morning."

"You were?"

"But you weren't home."

"I was there. The downstairs buzzer doesn't work sometimes."

"No, I got in. The doorman was on duty."

"Ah."

"I went up to your apartment and rang, Conrad."

21

"I feel terrible. I just didn't hear you."

"There was a pile of mail outside your door and two newspapers."

There was a pause.

"What were you doing there at that hour anyway?" he asked almost indignantly.

"I walked out on Fred today."

"I guess we should talk." He lowered his voice to a level suitable to the discussion of intimate affairs in crowded offices.

"Yes. We should talk."

"But not now," he said. "I'm just about to go into a meeting."

"*Of course*," I said, trying to sound as sarcastic as I possibly could.

"Why don't you just go on up to my house after work?"

"No, I'm not going to your house. I don't want to."

"You don't want to?"

"I think we'd better meet on neutral ground."

"I can tell you're very angry," he said sadly, "and very very upset. This is the first time I've made you angry. We could talk much better at my house really."

"No."

Somehow hearing from Conrad that I was angry and upset had made me begin to cry. I have always been undone by sympathy.

"I'll meet you in front of your building after work then." He was brisk now, all business. "Hi, Dianne. I'll be right with you." I could hear a commotion in the background, muffled voices. "Is that neutral enough?" he said.

Before I could answer he had hung up.

I waited for Conrad looking anxiously up Fourth Avenue, trying to catch sight of the Saab. I was amazed by the number of small green cars of various makes that passed me. I had never been aware there were so many of that particular shade. It reminded me of being pregnant and suddenly seeing other pregnant women all over the place—bellies moving toward me down every street.

He arrived slightly late, pulling over smoothly to the curb. "Heavy traffic," he said, opening the door for me. I got in next to him, displacing a pile of books and a half-eaten hero sandwich and putting them down on the floor behind my feet. "Why don't you throw those in the back?" Conrad said.

"It's okay."

He was studying me. I looked just once very quickly at his wonderfully blue eyes that were so richly fringed

23

with dark lashes. I looked away, clutching my small paper bag.

"Been shopping?" he said.

"Not exactly."

He smiled brilliantly for a moment. His hand brushed my knee as he started the car. I felt a flash of incongruous joy at being with him. I struggled to keep my anger intact, uninvaded.

He asked me if I wanted to go any place in particular.

"Anywhere," I said coldly.

"Let's just drive around then. I have another meeting in a couple of hours." He turned the corner and headed uptown. "Want to go through the park?"

"You sound like a cabdriver."

"I drove a cab for a while in '65. You didn't know that."

"Just one of the many things you've done."

"What's eating you, Molly?"

"I hate being lied to."

He sighed.

"You're not even good at it."

"That's true. Actually, I have a great respect for the truth. If I didn't, I'd be a much better liar, believe me. In some situations a lie is necessary."

"For example?" I said bitterly.

"For *example*," he said chidingly, shaking his head. "Do you know how much regard I have for you?" His voice was husky, slightly choked.

Tears rushed into my eyes, although it was love I would have preferred him to say.

He was looking straight at the traffic now. His hand moved on the wheel in a myriad of small adjustments.

"Conrad," I said, "are you involved with someone?"

"Involved?" With a deft swerve, the car shot ahead of a slow-moving bus. "*Involved*," Conrad said, "is a term

24

that hardly has any meaning. There are degrees of involvement. Are we involved—you and I?"

"Yes, I think we are."

"But what does that mean to you, Molly?"

"It means," I said with difficulty, the words catching in my throat, "that we care for each other."

"That is certainly the case." He turned now and beamed his smile at me. "Even though you care less for me right at this moment than you have at times in the past." His eyes changed from tender to slightly mischievous. "At any rate, I think involvement means more to you than you've said."

"Perhaps," I said unwillingly.

"No. Definitely. Don't think I don't know what you expect of me, Molly."

"I asked you a question before."

"Yes, you did. On the basis of what you found this morning when you turned up and I wasn't there."

"I can put two and two together."

"And much more than that, much much more. Molly, you're a thoroughly grown-up woman in most respects."

"In what respects am I not?"

"In your tendency to jump to conclusions."

"I see nothing ungrownup about that."

"But already, you see, you have me *involved* with someone you don't even know about."

"Well, aren't you?" I cried.

"Yes," he said defiantly, roughly, "I happened to be with a close friend last night. Yes, and the night before that too."

"Okay, Conrad! Okay!"

"You'll note that what I said was *with!*"

"Why couldn't you just say it in the first place?"

"Because I cared about how you heard it, goddamn it!"

We had both been shouting back and forth at each other in the little car. We looked at each other in amazement and fright. Conrad steered to the left and pulled over in front of a hydrant. I noticed beads of sweat on his face. Wet rings of hair were plastered to his forehead. I could see that he was suffering, that he must have felt humiliated. I would have if I had been him. His blue eyes looked at me pleadingly like my kid's did when I'd scolded him too hard. I almost took my hand and brushed his hair back from his forehead. I thought I was going mad with the anger and love all knotted up inside me and all that had happened to me that day and Conrad's tortuous logic going round in my head and confusing me further.

And now he began saying some things that were perfectly true. I couldn't argue with them. That all of us came into each other's lives from wherever it was we'd been before. That nothing was ever neat, especially for people who lived fully. We came to each other trailing old relationships, old attachments. "And who should know that better than you, Molly?"

I had an image of me dragging Fred into Conrad's life like an old vacuum cleaner gliding along on his little runners.

He said something too about nothing ever really being over, which didn't make too much of an impact on me at the time. I wanted only to get to what I thought was the point.

"And what about this attachment of yours, Conrad?"

I was determined that day to get the full story out of Conrad, however painful. Without information, how can one make choices? It was facts that I wanted. I made the mistake, however, of forgetting the importance of context. And Conrad was a master of that. He could spin a context out of himself like a great silken web.

The context in which he told me about the other woman in his life was an appeal for sympathy, my compassion for another frail and battered human, a sister if you like. I must confess, though, to having difficulties with the word *sister* in its all inclusive, non-filial sense. It is absolutely clear to me that there are some women who are my sisters and others who are definitely not. In this case I did not feel particularly sisterly, although I tried—guiltily aware of my political shortcomings.

This woman, my sister, was a modern dancer who'd become a dance therapist, who was now struggling toward a degree in psychology—which was only one of her problems. It was Conrad who had radicalized her, encouraged her to go to graduate school, to overcome the sense of intellectual inferiority that her disastrous marriage to a self-absorbed experimental filmmaker had left her with. Gradually he had been rebuilding her shattered sense of herself. His restoration was almost completed.

"Henry Higgins," I said.

He winced.

"I know you're angry, Molly. But if you could just see this woman, you'd understand."

"How do you know?" I said.

"Because you're not an unkind person."

I laughed painfully. "Maybe I'm not as kind as you think. Maybe I'm selfish, Conrad, about some things."

"Molly, I feel terribly responsible for Bobbie. I can't help it. She could be so easily destroyed just when things are beginning to open up for her. I can't just walk in on her and say, 'Listen, Bobbie, I've met someone else.' "

Oh yes you can, Conrad, I thought. You can go there tomorrow and say it.

He was going on now about her problems—some of which he hinted were sexual in nature, although he was unspecific about what they were. She had a tendency to panic, to become hysterical, enraged at the slightest provocations. He spoke of his suffering, the constant pressure he felt. It was hard to see why he stayed with her if she was as dreadful as he said.

"You haven't told her about us, I suppose."

"No," he said. "Of course I haven't. I think she senses something though."

"Senses something?"

"Sometimes she tells me that I seem different to her. I try very hard not to be."

"Is Bobbie a nickname or something?"

"Yes, it's short for Roberta."

"Roberta what?" I asked.

"Roberta Holloman. But why would you want to know that?"

"Because I'm going to be thinking about her a lot and I guess I want to know her name."

His face reddened in fury. "You're making it hard, Molly, harder than it needs to be." The words came out of him in a clenched kind of way. "Why would you want to think about her? What goes on between you and me has nothing to do with Roberta."

"You should have told me about her right at the beginning, Conrad, not kept it a secret! It isn't fair, Conrad. It isn't fair at all!"

"Would it have made a difference? Would you have decided to stay away from me?"

I looked at him. His blue eyes burned into mine. I could feel the heat between us that all this combat had brought on, a live kind of heat that invaded my flesh, vibrated against my skin.

"No, Conrad. It wouldn't have made any difference."

He pulled me to him then, crushing me against him. "Oh, Molly," he said.

Who isn't human?

Perhaps I should have walked out on Conrad, abandoned him to Roberta. The fact is that now I wanted him more than ever.

To many women—and I ruefully number myself among them—there is nothing more attractive than a strong man with weaknesses. There is something infinitely compelling in that contradiction. We see the man as an uncompleted work. It is we who will supply the finishing touches. Our belief in our wisdom and forebearance, our female hubris, are all too frequently either fatal or ridiculous—depending on one's angle of vision.

Feminists have only brought into the open a view of men that women have shared secretly all along. The truth is that we *expect* them to be frail creatures, rather than the reverse. And we excuse behavior in our men we would never permit ourselves or pardon in others of our kind. *That* is our peculiar double standard. We think of this as love.

Can you imagine the richness of conversation in a harem? Allowing for a certain amount of competition and jealousy among the concubines, imagine the delicious opportunities to pool certain observations about the pasha, to compare his performance with one to his performance with all the others—and perhaps see that they are the same. Surely in the process there would develop a highly sophisticated form of gallows humor. All this—and communal childcare as well!

But all these observations of course are hindsight. Returning to the scene in the Saab, where one of Conrad's solid thighs is wedged assertively between mine and his tongue is in my mouth and mine is in his and I run it along the edges of his sharp little teeth and feel everything cold and firm inside me melting away like so much sherbet, I see that my excuse-making mechanism has already started up, is in fact pumping away furiously because it has such an enormous amount of work to do. What it is coming up with very quickly is the image of Conrad as the victim of his own idealism. My Conrad, so sunny in his temperament, so unfailingly giving of himself to causes others would consider lost, had blundered into a situation where the zeal so admirable and appropriate in his professional life became a destructive element in his personal one. He was a man who could not resist an obligation. So it was Roberta's misery in fact that bound him to her! And I suspected that no one understood this better than Roberta did herself.

"Oh, Conrad," I said, disengaging my mouth from his for a moment, "I'm so tired of being miserable. I'd just like to be happy for a change. Wouldn't you?" Since I knew there was no way I could compete with Roberta, what I was doing was offering a contrast.

30

"We're happy together a lot of the time," Conrad said, struggling with his left hand to unhook the back of my bra.

"But I don't want to be happy in bits. I want it to be a continuum." The bra came loose under my shirt and flapped against my skin, its stiff nylon lace grazing my nipples. Conrad's hand came around from behind, lifted the fabric away and took a breast.

"I love your tits," he said. He squeezed gently, then a little too hard. "You're very sensitive there, aren't you?"

I became afraid of losing my train of thought. "Yes," I whispered faintly.

"I think you're sensitive all over." He bit my ear. His right hand began to undo the middle buttons on my shirt. I began to feel more undressed than if I were naked.

"Conrad, we're on Madison Avenue."

"I'm seizing some moments of happiness for myself. I've had a hard day. Besides, the windows are very dirty."

"Conrad, I'm serious about what I was saying before."

"I know you are."

"What I mean was I thought you and I could be happy. I think we really have a chance."

"No one can be truly happy in a capitalist society," he reminded me sternly, plunging his face between my breasts. I held him to me, my fingers playing with his wonderful hair, twisting it into little red ringlets and letting them spring away from me, as his mouth moved eagerly upon my flesh.

For some reason, I was reminded of the scene at the very end of *The Grapes of Wrath*, where Rose of Sharon, the young nursing mother, gives the starving man her breast. I hadn't read it since junior high school but it had made a lasting impression on me.

31

"Conrad, are you listening? I was referring to the possibility of a private happiness."

"Uh huh," he said. His knee burrowed in between my legs and I clasped my trembling thighs around him, staring over his shoulder at the hydrant, the bottom halves of pedestrians passing as if in a dream. I thought of Roberta and her unstated sexual problems. I thought of Fred eating a hamburger alone in Max's Kansas City. He orders it medium and gets it well done. Morosely he eats one French fry after another and leaves the pickle. He scans the bar for an available long-legged beauty but it is full of businessmen drinking Martinis. And then I stopped thinking of anything but how I could go on and on with Conrad just like this.

Since the car could no longer be considered neutral territory, we went to Conrad's apartment after all, rushing there in such a hurry that Conrad parked the Saab illegally and found it towed away when he got up the next morning. I went into the bedroom and took off my clothes while Conrad made an important phone call. He had asked me if I would mind changing the linen on the bed and gave me a set of sheets provided by his mother. They were printed with little daisies. As old as he was, his mother still bought him all his underwear, socks and linens. The sheets that were on the bed had a palmtree motif. I wondered if he had lain on them with Roberta. I stripped them off and threw them in the corner.

In the next room I could hear Conrad canceling his meeting. He was telling someone that a crisis had come up and he had to go to Detroit. "But, baby," I thought I heard him say. However, it might have been my imagination.

I was suddenly very tired and a little depressed. I spread out the clean sheets and waited.

It's six o'clock in the morning again, and this time she's in a taxi headed downtown, trying to get home before Fred wakes up.

There is not much traffic. The streets have a clean, bare look to them. The sky is rather pale, as if there will be rain later. In the twenties there are trucks delivering flowers. She wonders what it would be like to live in the flower district. Already she has a sense of homelessness that is surprisingly exhilarating. She has been rooted in a small and stunted place. It is time for her to move on. Later perhaps she'll buy a newspaper, look at the ads for apartments.

Just why she's going downtown this morning, aside from the fact that her clothes are there, is not quite clear. It seems the thing to do. She has begun to operate by a whole new set of rules. She makes them up as she goes along. Last night, for example, it suddenly seemed no longer conceivable to go, as she'd been going all along,

33

ever since her affair with Conrad began, from Conrad's bed to her husband's.

Around one A.M. when the clock radio Conrad had set awakened them, she'd announced that she was going to stay. He'd seemed a little alarmed—and she was somewhat surprised herself by this decision. "Is that wise?" he'd asked. "It's okay," she'd reassured him, "I know what I'm doing." Even though she didn't know. She was improvising, really. She'd made Conrad lie down again and wrapped herself around him. He'd tossed restlessly for a while, but had finally fallen asleep. She herself had been sleepless, her mind racing with excited, disconnected thoughts. She'd left when it became light, tucking the blanket she'd disarranged around his shoulders and whispering, "Don't get up."

Her absolute failure to consider consequences will seem rather strange to her later. She actually had the idea that Fred would not particularly notice her absence, since he took so little notice of her in general. How could it matter to him whether she was in or out? Either she'd find him asleep when she arrived or not yet back himself from the night's adventures.

She stares out the window at the familiar neighborhood below Fourteenth Street as the cab speeds down Seventh Avenue. She directs the driver to turn right on Christopher Street and has him let her out on the corner of the block where she lives. She crosses the street to the local newsstand and buys a paper. She tries to remember whether they have run out of anything. Catfood? Coffee? Liquid detergent? For a moment she thinks of going to the all-night delicatessen around the corner, returning with groceries. She realizes she is a little nervous. It is an unfamiliar situation.

She lets herself into her building and goes quietly up

the stairs. She digs her key out of her pocket and slips it into the lock. She listens and hears nothing. Then she opens the door.

To her great astonishment all the lights in the house are on. And Fred is up, he is fully dressed, he is just getting to his feet in the tiny dining alcove where, judging by the litter of ashtrays and coffee cups on the table, he has spent a good part of the night. He rushes at her and knocks her to the floor. "Whore!" he yells.

In my fifth year of marriage I met a man through my work. He was a professor of economics from Milwaukee who was writing a three-part reconsideration of Thorstein Veblen for *New Thought*. He was an older man, in his late forties, who had a certain blond, perpetually innocent look that I always associate with the Midwest. His sentence structure was beyond belief—dreadful agglutinations of words in which there lurked flashes of theoretical brilliance. I sat with him for days, shearing away dependent clauses that were not attached to anything and suggesting ways they could be made to have independent existences of their own. He was abjectly grateful—particularly so when the essays were published and his colleagues praised his clarity of expression. He was not the first writer I worked with who fell a little bit in love with my pencil. Nor was he the last. He would insist on taking me out to long lunches in the middle of our work sessions. Just before he went back to Milwaukee, he told me I reminded him of his favorite high school English teacher, Miss Metcalf.

I was depressed by this association. I went to the ladies' room and inspected my face for signs of severity and age, for any hint of asexuality. I would not have been shocked to have found the latter—such were my relations with my husband at the time.

I was therefore considerably surprised when the phone in my office rang three weeks later. It was the economist. "Hello, Miss Metcalf," he said. "I'm back in town." He asked me if I were free that evening, explaining that he was attending an economists' convention and was staying at the Howard Johnson Motor Inn, where he wished us to meet and have cocktails. I was so totally unprepared for this kind of invitation, after my years of faithfulness to Fred, that I was thrown into a kind of tongue-tied panic. I collected myself after a moment and invited him home to dinner. He hesitated and then accepted. "That's real nice of you," he said.

It was a rather peculiar evening. First, Fred was very critical of me for allowing my "work" to follow me home. He told me he fully expected to be bored, since most writers he had met socially were both dull and opinionated, and he detested the thought of being trapped into the role of host. Second, my child had an upset stomach and called out to me in heartrending tones all through the meal and finally ran out into the living room and vomited on the *flokati* rug. I ran back and forth between the kitchen, the dining table and my child with food and buckets of water and hardly got in a word of conversation. Fortunately, the two men discovered they had a mutual interest in football—one that I did not share. By ten o'clock, when I was finally able to sit down, I was exhausted. Meaningless fragments of discussion about the Green

Bay Packers buzzed in my ears until my eyes finally closed and I drifted off into a humiliating sleep.

I thought I'd seen the last of the economist. But he turned up at my office the following day just before noon. He looked flushed and troubled. He implored me to go to lunch with him. As we waited for the elevator he gave me a clumsy kiss, springing away afterward with mumbled apologies. As we sat a few minutes later in the Szechuan restaurant around the corner, he confessed to having contracted a hopeless passion for me, not unlike the one he'd had for Miss Metcalf when he was an adolescent boy. I was touched. I let him squeeze and knead my fingers upon the plastic upholstery of the booth. His tweed-covered leg pressed tentatively against mine beneath the table cloth. I sat stock still and unresistant, feeling only the slightest response—perhaps because it was a relationship in which I so clearly had the upper hand. I told him I would never be unfaithful to my husband. He said he understood. He wanted only to keep seeing me under any circumstances.

The affair, if you can call it that, went on for nearly nine months. The economist and I would meet whenever he came to town and have lunch in various ethnic restaurants, where we would enjoy the limited physical contact permitted by the decor. He never asked me to the Howard Johnson Motor Inn again. In a way I was disappointed by this lack of spirit on his part as much as I was relieved. In between his visits I tended to forget him— being reminded of the fact that I lived in his imagination by an occasional picture postcard addressed to Miss Metcalf and signed "Fondly, Stewart." At any rate, he was adequate in his role as my secret admirer. A more tangible and demanding one would have terrified me. At the time I still had thoughts of saving my marriage.

In the spring of that year an epidemic of chicken pox

swept like wildfire through the Robin Dell nursery school. My son succumbed early with a mild case, requiring incessant doses of apple juice and television. I was not so fortunate. When the incubation period ended, itching blisters burst forth on every inch of my flesh. My husband shunned me as if I were a leper, averting his eyes as I sat across from him at meals and even suggesting we eat at separate tables. His offended esthetic sensibility drove him to the bars earlier in the evenings than ever before and often kept him out until dawn. I would paint myself with calomine lotion and lie itching and weeping upon my bed, questioning my very existence. It was one of several times in my life that I have reached almost absolute despair in circumstances that others might objectively consider ludicrous. But my sufferings, my grief, as I lay in that lonely apartment, were very real. I knew without a doubt that my husband did not love me, that if my affliction were permanent Fred would disappear from my life. I looked in the mirror at my pocked and swollen face that seemed to belong to a stranger and imagined myself irrevocably scarred, abandoned by my husband without so much as a get-well card. I knew I would heal and that our normal life together would resume with its attendant apathy—but I no longer had hope of anything more. It is in the death of hope that one begins finally to let go—in the perception of an underlying pattern that repeats and repeats and will repeat again.

It seems odd to me now that I ever shed a tear for Fred or for the kind of life that we had together. Perhaps I was really mourning the approaching end of my own inertia, and my tears were those of a coward. At any rate, for days they flowed from me like recycled water from a fountain, running down my loathsome blistered cheeks and making them itch all the more from the salt they left behind them.

It was in such a mood that I heard the doorbell ring one afternoon. Hurriedly wiping my eyes on the edge of my sheet and throwing my decrepit quilted bathrobe around me, I went to the door to let in what I thought was the delivery man from the A&P. Instead I found the economist. I learned later that he'd turned up at the office that morning and was told I was sick, but not the nature of my illness. Perhaps the thought of appearing on my doorstep as I lay on my sickbed in slightly feverish *déshabillé* had inflamed in him the last flickering of his original intention. He was carrying what looked like a bottle of wine in a paper bag and a small bouquet of anemones. He stared at me in dismayed confusion as if he were trying to place me. "Go away," I croaked. "I have the chicken pox." I closed the door in his face and sank laughing wildly into the nearest chair until once more I began to weep.

I never saw the economist again, except in my most strictly professional capacity.

As I lay sprawled on the floor that morning, with my husband towering above me like a righteous and avenging archangel, I reflected rapidly upon our history and decided that the epithet he'd given me was undeserved. As was his assault upon a person admittedly so much smaller than himself. We seemed like actors in a Victorian melodrama rather than an average Village couple swept along by the Sexual Revolution. I lay there on the rug rather calmly, considering the shock of his attack. No one had tried to beat me up since I was nine years old.

He was shouting now, his face fiery and contorted. I had never heard him express such strong emotion. I listened to his enraged description of his tormented, sleepless night, how he'd tossed and turned in the bed I had so cynically deserted, how he'd finally risen and paced, how he'd imagined me in various poses in the lurid embrace

41

of Conrad Schwartzberg. "You fucking lied to me!" he yelled.

Which was true. While I'd told Fred about Conrad at the very beginning—I suppose because I needed to show him that some other man could desire me—I'd had to promise the affair was over in order to be able to get out of the house on certain nights to carry it on.

"You weren't off raising your consciousness somewhere with a bunch of women. You were getting laid! You were getting laid! Right?"

"Yes," I said. "I was getting laid."

Fred lifted his fist as if to strike me again, but instead brought it crashing down on the Formica table top. The dishes there made a small but distinct clink of apprehension. With a fierce cry and an impatient sweep of his wrist, he cleared them to the ground.

I raised myself cautiously on one elbow. "You're being unreasonable," I said.

"Don't tell me what's unreasonable!"

"But you don't even want me," I reminded him. "You don't, really."

How coolly now I could state the fact that a year ago had immobilized me, left me sobbing into my pillow. I thought my consciousness had indeed undergone a change.

I regard myself as I was that momentous day, wondering at my dangerous innocence. Even Fred's blow left nothing more than a bruise upon my chin. I burned with clarity like an incandescent bulb. The future I would have with Conrad shimmered almost within reach, lush and inviting. I had only to endure the last bleak stretch of the past and to skirt the small obstacle that Roberta represented. She was not included in my vision of the future.

I was leaving a desert and entering a swamp. But no one could have persuaded me of that or deflected my path.

There is such a thin line for women between adventure and misadventure. It is still hard for us to be heroes in the active, external sense of, say, climbing mountains, hopping freights. We tend to be heroes of our own imaginations. I am as much idiot as heroine, perhaps more the former than the latter—an educated dope, as my mother would say, having earned her right to pass judgment by her investment in my tuition.

Nonetheless, I like to remember how invincible I felt as I left my old life. I was so unquestionably in the right that nothing very bad could happen to me. I had even taken it upon myself to become the bearer of the truth. No more lies to anyone, no more shabby excuses. I had been as guilty of those, for the sake of expedience, as my husband and my lover. How could I ask Conrad not to lie to me if I demonstrated each time I slipped away to see him how well I could lie myself, as well as the strength of the hold my husband still had upon me?

I got to my feet and brushed myself off. I said something to Fred I will always recall with profound satisfaction: "I've had a hundred nights like the one you've had. And you've had only one."

He was silent for a moment as the truth of this observation struck home. I think he knew as well as I did that a hundred was a very low estimate. I wondered how many nights there'd really been, and attempted to multiply the average of two or three a week by the number of years we'd been together.

"But you're my wife," he said finally, almost plaintively. "You're supposed to be my wife."

43

I walked past him to the bedroom where I retrieved the purse I'd forgotten the day before and put some things into a small suitcase. I walked past him again to the front door as he stood, still wrestling with the double standard.

"Don't think you can come back, you little whore!" I heard him shout behind me as I left for good.

First impressions have a curious strength. They grip the imagination tenaciously. They are half-composed of physical bits of evidence—a warm voice, an understanding word, a soft look in the eyes—and half the creatures of our own minds entirely, our own desires and needs at a given moment. We tend to make up the people we fall in love with.

I still remember with some wistfulness the initially appealing boyish irresponsibility of Fred, just as I remember the day an outrageously brash person named Conrad Schwartzberg walked into the office of *New Thought*, talked to me for two hours about how the magazine could be made more politically relevant, made several long distance phone calls without asking my permission, and finally fell silent and stared at me and said, "I'm going to see you again. I like your sensibility." I see us hurrying around a certain corner in the Village only a few weeks afterward and falling upon each other in a kind of desperate passion—knowing we have exactly twenty minutes to be together before I must pick up my groceries and go home, arriving a little later than usual, which I will blame on the subway. We cling together and kiss right there on Eleventh Street off Seventh Avenue between a barbershop and a bakery. I think that was the day Conrad said he couldn't stand to think of me going back to Fred each time, and he asked if I'd ever think of living with him in the country or having another child. And I told him I could if everything were right— although the truth was that the idea of living in the country, even with Conrad, scared the hell out of me. I knew that after a few months with the trees, I'd have a perverse craving for cement. But naturally the invitation meant everything to me, and I probably would have gone and tried it out if he'd really meant it and become a bread-baker and raised my own zucchini and produced as many redheaded babies as he wanted. I think it was Vermont that he had in mind.

It was, however, to a four-room apartment on West Eighty-sixth Street that I moved myself and Matthew, my five-year-old son, much sooner than either Conrad or I had ever expected. Too soon, perhaps. It's hard to say. Timing is an important but mysterious factor in relationships.

There were eight blocks between Conrad's apartment and mine. You walked to Columbus Avenue and turned right, passing the rear of the Museum of Natural History, various secondhand carpet stores and vegetable stands where the vegetables also had a certain secondhand look, a bicycle shop, the laundromat where Conrad was said to do his laundry, and then turned right again on Seventy-eighth Street. You could do it in fifteen minutes. By car we were exactly five minutes apart—with maybe another twenty to find a parking space. In other words, we were not widely separated geographically. We were close enough for Conrad to get out of bed at my place and go home for a clean shirt, close enough for spur-of-the-moment walks, for hot impulsive midnight visits. I realized almost immediately, though, that Conrad was in a state of retreat.

Fortunately, I was too distracted to dwell upon it much. If running way from home were a simpler matter, I am sure many more people would do it. If you are thirty-five years old and the mother of a small precocious boy with a collection of three hundred comics, eight shoeboxes of baseball cards, five hundred Wacky Package stickers, four ventriloquist dolls, a turtle, two cats and a complete set of electric trains, you are not exactly free as a cloud. The fact is, you must speedily live in a reasonable facsimile of the place you have just left, and must rapidly acquire a landlord, a moving van and accounts with the phone and electric companies. I accomplished all of the above in two days flat just before Matthew came back from his vacation in the Catskills with my mother.

Conrad came over in the evening of the day I moved in. I hadn't seen him since the morning I'd gone home to Fred. He seemed strangely subdued, walking around the premises warily like a cat inspecting a new environment. I'd been up since five o'clock that morning and was covered with plaster dust. Even while he was there, I kept on frantically spackling holes and cracks, since it was my intention to paint the entire apartment myself that weekend, excluding the ceilings because I was too short to reach them with a roller and the highest step on the ladder has always made me nervous.

47

"Well, you really did it," he said.

"You sound as though you don't quite believe it."

"It's just that I need time to assimilate so much change." He sat down upon a box.

I laughed. I was feeling pleased with myself. "*You* need time!"

"I suppose I was the catalyst," he observed gloomily.

"Oh Conrad, you're much more than the catalyst." Holding my trowel of spackle above his head, I kissed him precariously. I felt he needed reassurance. No one likes to be just a catalyst for someone else. The front of him was white where I'd pressed against him. I put down my trowel. "Let me dust you off," I said tenderly.

"No need." He got up and paced around for a while. "I suppose it was bound to happen anyway," he said.

"What was?"

"Your leaving. I suppose it was just a question of time."

I put a dab of spackle into a hole the size of a quarter and took a long time smoothing it down with a kitchen knife. "What are you trying to say, Conrad?" I asked finally.

"I just don't want to be held responsible." He laughed uncomfortably.

"You're not responsible. Okay?"

"You would have done it anyway."

"In time."

"I did tell you not to stay over. You have an impulsive streak, you know."

"You disapprove of that?"

He sat down on the box again and began to run his hands through his hair. "I have so many pressures. So many pressures right at this moment."

"I don't intend to be one of them, Conrad."

"I have to be in court first thing on Monday and I have to spend all weekend working on the brief. And there's a Marxist study group in Rockaway that's invited me to be a guest speaker. Also, my mother is depressed and I have to go over there for dinner . . . "

"Poor Conrad."

"You don't understand. Your life is relatively simple."

"Simple!" I exclaimed.

He looked away embarrassed. "Well, it will be—once you get all this moving straightened out."

"What about Roberta? How's she doing?" I inquired blandly.

"Oh, she's fine this week."

"So she's not one of your pressures."

"Molly, there's a tone in your voice when you speak of Roberta— Perhaps it's not a subject that should be open to discussion between us."

I was careful not to mention Roberta again that evening, or the next time Conrad and I saw each other, which was nearly a week later. When I'd inquired after her health, I wouldn't have been at all sorry to learn that the earth had opened and swallowed her up.

I looked up Roberta's name in the phone book one day. There was a *Holloman, R.* on Central Park West. Further downtown in the Village, on Bank Street, there was a *Holloman, Theodore.* I decided that he must be her ex-husband. I could not imagine her having been married to *Holloman, Oscar,* who lived on Mother Cabrini Boulevard in Washington Heights. I wondered if Theodore's friends called him Ted, just as Conrad called her Bobbie. Bobbie and Ted. I was not surprised she had not put her full name in the phone book; she was prudent enough as a single woman to want to avoid nuisance calls. Despite

49

what Conrad had told me, I felt she was a woman who could ultimately take care of herself. I pictured her striding through Central Park in her dancer's body with her dog, if she had one. She is wearing a leotard, jeans, colorful espadrilles and no makeup; the wind tosses her hair which is probably loose and down at least to her shoulders. She is okay—not beautiful but okay. I see her entering the typical West Side lobby of her building, nodding to the doorman. The dog is somehow no longer with her. She is carrying a shopping bag from the health food store and a plant in a small pot—a fern. She arches and flexes her foot as she waits for the elevator, studies her pointed toe. She goes upstairs to wait for Conrad.

I feel I am guilty of spying on her and since I am already guilty, I call her up.

She picks up the phone in the middle of the second ring, much faster than I expected.

"Hello." She has a girlish voice, a little breathy. "Hello?"

"Oh. Is this JK5-2643?"

"No it isn't," she answers crisply.

"I'm sorry," I say. "I think I have the wrong—"

She hangs up before I finish my sentence. I add impatience to what I already know of her.

I am trembling a little. I wonder if I have just done something wicked. I am not entirely displeased at the thought.

An odd thing happened, one of those peculiar crossings of lines that wouldn't have been particularly startling to me except for the circumstances. Having lived in the city all my life, I took it for granted that if you moved in certain intersecting circles you would ultimately learn that everyone was connected to everyone else. You had only to become sensitized to a particular name to find it cropping up even in the most unexpected places.

I had an old friend I hadn't seen for months. I lived very close to Deborah now that I had moved, and I called to give her my new address as well as to tell her about the other developments in my life. I gave her a brief account of the saga of Fred and Conrad and Roberta, and she said, "Oh, but you know her!"

"I know her?"

"Don't you remember? I introduced you. It was two summers ago, when you and Fred were in Amagansett. You came over to the house and visited."

"I can remember that much."

"Well, Bobbie was there. She was one of the people I was sharing the house with. Don't you remember the woman who was very depressed because her husband had just gone off to Brazil with someone else?"

I thought suddenly that I did. It was the word *Brazil* that began to summon her up again for me.

"Do you ever run into her?" I asked.

"Actually I see her every week. We're in the same exercise class. She seems very different lately, much more outgoing, talks a lot about being radicalized."

"Conrad's influence," I said. "Does she talk much about him?"

There was a moment of silence on the other end of the phone. "Listen," Deborah said, "Bobbie's sort of a friend of mine, not a close friend, but still . . . I mean it isn't quite fair . . . "

"You're right," I said quickly.

"I'm sorry, Molly. It sounds like both of you are in a messy situation, which is not exactly what either of you needs. *Men!*" she said bitterly. "I just don't want to be in the middle. Okay?"

51

I told her I understood.

The conversation remained in my mind. I went over everything Deborah had said, combing it for significance. Conrad's involvement with Roberta seemed more of a fact to me now, more fleshed out and tangible, not just something I had heard about. It existed as a fact for others, too, it commanded its own loyalties. Deborah had favored neither of us—her old tie to me was counterbalanced by her desire to behave correctly. Perhaps she even disapproved of me, thought I was in the wrong, that I should give Conrad up. I had thought of Roberta as the Other Woman, the interloper, even though it was she who had known Conrad first. Perhaps I was the interloper myself. It was not a role I wished to play. I wanted to be right. It was disturbing to think that I might not be, that as much as I wanted and needed Conrad I perhaps had no claim to him. And yet it was Conrad who had come to me, not I who had lured him away. He had his needs as well. His mistake had been his attempt to keep me from the truth.

I tried to remember Roberta as I'd seen her that day two summers ago when she'd seemed so incidental to my life I'd forgotten even her name immediately. I attempted to reconstruct the scene of our meeting—the knotty pine walls of that living room in Amagansett, the white cane furniture, the orange Indian print spread on the couch. I remembered eating a pumpernickel bagel. Had it been a Sunday brunch Fred and I had gone to? Yes, people were sitting on the floor in bathing suits with plates in their laps, talking and drinking coffee. And someone said, "Where's Bobbie?" And a woman in a purple caftan said, "I don't think she wants to get up." And I heard someone else say something about Brazil. But at some point later she came out of one of the bedrooms, and the woman in the purple caftan rushed over to her and asked her how she was and led her to the couch with the Indian print spread and got a plate of food for her which she didn't eat.

I remembered all that now, and how I tried not to look at her much because she looked so awful. I remembered a reddened, tear-sodden face and long tangled black hair which the woman in the purple caftan insisted on brushing, and some other people coming over to Bobbie and insisting that she go sailing with them. But she remained just as miserable. And when someone—Deborah—introduced us, she'd looked off into the distance as though she didn't see me.

I wondered if I would even recognize her now that she was outgoing and radicalized—more like the dancer i had imagined but still with that core of misery that commanded such solicitude from others, that bound Conrad to her in a way it was difficult to understand, the buoyancy and energy in him drawn to that inert figure I'd seen on the couch—which was the side of herself I was sure she consistently showed him.

She is happy on Tuesdays and Fridays and anxious the rest of the week. It is on Tuesdays and Fridays that she sees him. Sometimes a late Sunday night becomes free at the last minute. He says they are seeing each other two or three times as much as they did before.

She would like to be like a friend of hers whose idea of a perfect relationship is to have an affair with a man who lives in a different part of the country and to meet with him once a month in a city somewhere in between. Another friend rides around on a bicycle picking up an occasional stranger. It would embarrass her if either of them knew how much time she spends waiting for Conrad. Even on the nights when she is not going to see him, she feels in a state of suspension, as if she is not quite real to herself. Why should she need his presence to animate her?

He's always later than he says he's going to be. If it's at

ten that she expects him, he will arrive at midnight; if it's at eight, he will come at nine-thirty and then she'll have to contend with Matthew who has insisted on staying up for Conrad's visit and is by that time nearly hysterical with exhaustion and will not go to sleep even after Conrad has wrestled him a few times and carried him slung over his shoulders to his bed. But she likes the way that he is with the boy. It's one of the things she likes best about him now—and he knows it, grinning at her over Matthew's head when he catches her noticing the way they are together. Matthew always asks her whether Conrad is coming over. "Well, why isn't he here *yet?*" he asks indignantly.

Sometimes by the time Conrad comes, she's very angry. Although she's spent three days waiting for him, the extra hour or so added on by his lateness is almost unendurable. Sometimes she nearly hates him and contemplates not answering the doorbell, letting him ring and ring. If it wasn't for Matthew, she'd certainly go out. Yes, she'd go out and walk, visit a friend, have a drink somewhere, leave a terse and pointed note:

Too bad you're too late this time.

M.

Fuck him anyway. She'd walk off into the night and take a taxi to another part of town.

But when he is actually there in all his smiling bigness, she is just mostly very glad to see him. That is the paradox. And she ends up feeling so sorry for him too on certain nights when he arrives on her doorstep exhausted and pale, breathing hard—with tales of a meeting that went on for six hours, or a flat tire on the Jersey Turnpike, and it turns out the poor man has not even had dinner. She rushes to the kitchen eager to nourish him. "Just

56

something light," he sighs, sinking down onto one of her rickety kitchen chairs, and ends up eating all her leftovers—half a chicken, an entire bowl of potato salad, the remains of a brie.

Sometimes, singing union songs, he takes a shower in her bathroom and washes his hair with her shampoo, Dr. Brunner's Peppermint Soap—the label of which shows a fiercely bearded man and says you can use Dr. Brunner's for cleaning your teeth or washing your dog and any other known hygienic purpose.

It is a few weeks before she dares to buy him a toothbrush. It is a red one that she selects for him, and she presents it to him rather shyly: "Here's something I think you need." "Oh thanks," he says matter-of-factly, without much interest. It is clear that this is just a toothbrush to him rather than a significant toothbrush. She puts it in the holder with her yellow one and Matthew's green one and looks on it with pleasure on the mornings when he has stayed over and with bitter regret when it is unused.

Sometimes I asked myself what I wanted—which I knew wasn't the same as what I was supposed to want. I was supposed to want freedom. The runaway wife was the new cultural phenomenon, celebrated in everything from poems whose lines mixed kitchen imagery with menstrual blood to how-to articles in the women's magazines. Now I was free—free to have as many lovers as I wanted of whichever sex or to live with a vibrator in celibacy, free to go to rap sessions any night of the week if I could afford a baby-sitter, or to develop my mind in night classes at the New School for Social Research and my dormant strength in Roberta's exercise classes, free to start an exciting career—but I had already been working all of my adult life.

What I did was eat out a lot—sampling the various restaurants up and down Broadway with my son. For a while almost every evening that I wasn't expecting Conrad we were out *à deux,* my patient child with his shopping bag of comics and small plastic monsters with which he would relieve the boredoom of a televisionless dinner and I with whatever manuscript I happened to be reading. We would look around us and invariably see a number of similar couples at other tables even on weekdays. I taught Matthew to eat with chopsticks and he was soon on intimate terms with the waiters in our favorite Szechuan restaurant, who put cherries in his cokes and plied him with fortune cookies. Even so he yearned for Burger King and a power struggle developed between us, which he won.

After a few nights of concession, I went back to standing on line at the supermarket after work and home cooking accompanied by the shrieks and grunts of the Flintstones.

As delightful as small children are, they are not necessarily the best companions for adults. Our tastes and preoccupations are not the same. I had, for example, no appreciation for the monsters that were Matthew's passion at the time. As much as he sought my opinions as to their respective merits, I could tell him only that I preferred the elegance of Dracula to the essential klutziness of Frankenstein and felt total indifference as to Hulk. This was my unchanging position on the subject.

"But what about Godzilla?" he asked me one evening for the forty-first time as I brooded upon my life as a single parent, my accumulation of debts, my suspicion that Roberta was as firmly fixed in Conrad's life as ever.

"I'm afraid I just don't think about him at all."

"So you like Hulk more?"

"Sure," I said.

"You're not even listening, Mom! You're not even listening! You said you didn't *like* Hulk last week."

His small face trembled with hurt and indignation and I gathered him in my arms. "Listen," I said, rubbing my cheek against his silky hair, "I've got things on my mind."

"What things?"

"Nothing you'd understand, honey"

"Well, I've got a right to know everything you're thinking because you're my mother."

"No," I said firmly, "nobody has that right about anybody else."

"You wanna know what I'm thinking?" he offered.

"If you want to tell me."

"Well, I'm thinking that you're thinking that Conrad isn't your best friend enough. Otherwise he'd have more sleepovers at our house."

I hastily abandoned my introspection, got out a monster comic and read it to him until Conrad arrived, on time for a change. "Oh Conrad!" Matthew said, running up and giving him a little kiss. "What on earth are you doing here so early?"

I remember it was a Friday night in October and I'd been living on Eighty-sixth Street a little over a month. Conrad was just back from a trip and seemed particularly cheerful, more relaxed than I'd seen him for a while. He insisted on taking over the reading of the comic, which he read with far more dramatic effect than I had ever attempted, and afterward he agreed to be Frankenstein for ten minutes and chased Matthew around the apartment while Matthew fended him off with the plant-mister.

I sat in the living room as the chase went on, listening to Conrad's heavy footsteps and Matthew's light, running ones, his screams of delight. I felt an odd sadness, a

59

suspicious teariness of the kind that comes over me sometimes when I watch reruns of *The Wizard of Oz* or *Miracle on Thirty-fourth Street.* It is the theme of reunion or reintegration that I identify with so strongly, the orphan coming home at last. I remember thinking, "Why can't things be like this?"—which was absurd, because things were indeed "like this" at that particular moment. It was real life I was watching this time.

There is no doubt in my mind that what I was experiencing just then was an attack of nostalgia for the nuclear family—that it was this outmoded configuration I wished to impose on my relationship with Conrad. Despite the lessons of my recent history, I was only waiting for the opportunity to make the attempt again. It was not so much an image of traditional marriage and family that I had but one of an idealized unity—a stubborn vision that I had never lost, that I pursued then and always will pursue.

I remember we put Matthew to bed together, making him ready like a small pharaoh for his journey into the night, his ventriloquist dolls on either side of his pillow, the bear he'd had nearly all his life propped up against the wall, his Batman cape folded at the foot of his bed in case he should need it. After I had kissed him, he pulled Conrad's head down to him with his strong little pajamaed arms, and not too long after that we went to bed ourselves.

Something gave way in me that night—as if there'd been a small barrier inside me that I'd been almost unaware of until Conrad broke through, reaching now into the deepest places, exploring my most secret caverns with a freedom I had somehow never permitted him before. "That was fantastic," he whispered afterward, as I lay weeping for joy beside him. "I love you," I said. He didn't answer, just lay there very quietly. It was so nearly dark in the room that I could hardly see his face. After a while he took my hand and squeezed it, crushing my fingers until I thought the bones would snap.

He was asleep before I even realized it. I lay still feeling him inside me, as if my body, my sex, had its own kind of memory. I only wanted him again. I put my hand on him at last, almost guiltily, because I knew he was a man who needed his sleep, holding and caressing the part of him I loved so much until it swelled and grew firm and he turned to me and put it in me.

Perhaps I was too conscious of what I wanted to repeat. It wasn't quite as good the second time. Nonetheless, I woke up as soon as it became light the next morning with the conviction that everything was about to change.

I remember lying there next to Conrad for what might have been an hour, thinking of the words he'd said to me the night before and how he'd clasped my hand. His arm was resting heavily upon my ribs, but I was careful not to shift under the weight of it. Turning my head slightly, I stared at his face—the thick eyelashes, the slightly open mouth, the small white scar upon his chin, the sweat glistening upon his forehead. There was a luxurious freedom in being conscious while he slept.

I wished he would sleep on and on. At least I'd know that he was there. When he woke up, his thoughts would be of leaving. I wondered if this time, though, he might stay—if now he could begin to break with Roberta. I could feel a dangerous impatience rising up in me. I wanted this weekend with him.

The bedroom door opened suddenly and there was a

blare of Saturday morning cartoons from the living room. Matthew came to my bedside bearing his cats, whom he'd thoughtfully brought along for my amusement.

"What are you doing here?" I whispered fiercely, hastily pulling the covers around me.

"Mom, I want some cereal."

"Well, go and get it."

"I want you to do it."

"Matthew, you're perfectly capable of putting some cereal in a bowl and pouring milk on it. Go on now."

Conrad stirred and muttered something unintelligible. The arm he had flung across me jerked away.

"Matthew!" I hissed.

He stood there looking at me reproachfully, his pink lower lip protruding. He released the cats who skittered across the room and stretched himself out next to me on the edge of the bed.

"Please, Matthew."

He lay there determined to be unmoveable, beating his heels against the mattress. On the floor at the foot of the bed, the cats had discovered Conrad's shoes and were playing with the laces.

"You're being very naughty," I said sternly.

"No I'm not," he said with all the confidence of someone who had mastered the art of passive resistance at the age of five. But even if I had been able to send him away, it was too late. Conrad stretched and rolled from side to side. His eyelids fluttered open. "Hi, Conrad," Matthew said.

Shaking his head groggily, Conrad sat up. 'What time is it?" he said.

"The big hand is on the three and the little hand is on the eight," Matthew announced proudly.

"Eight fifteen." With a groan, Conrad sank down again. "I should go soon," he said.

I felt a slight constriction in my throat. "Why should you go so early? It's Saturday."

"I have so much to catch up with. I might as well take advantage of getting an early start."

Reaching under the covers, I put my hand upon his side, moving it gently up and down, slowly increasing the pressure of my fingers. His eyes half-closed. "Mm, that feels good," he said.

I could feel my heart beating as if I were about to do something risky. "Why don't you go back to sleep and I'll go out to Broadway in a while and get some bagels?"

"You know me. I never eat breakfast."

"Wanna wrestle, Conrad?" Matthew asked hopefully.

"Matthew, I want you to get off the bed this instant!"

One of the cats jumped up and walked across Conrad's chest. "I might as well get up now," he said. Under the circumstances I could hardly blame him.

I gave Matthew an angry push. "Now just get up and get the cats out of here and go in and eat some cereal."

"You're real mean today, Mom," he said, sliding to the floor.

I assured him I was going to get meaner if he didn't obey, and wondered miserably what impression this demonstration of shrewish behavior was making on Conrad. It was clear, however, that it had very little effect upon my son. Far from leaving the room, he wandered over to the window and began playing with the window shade, jerking it experimentally to see how far it would roll up.

"He's impossible this morning," I said to Conrad.

Conrad laughed. "I think he's being normal. At least he's not developing an authoritarian personality. It's just the early morning television that gets to me."

"I hear every word you're saying, you big smarty," Matthew said.

65

"So what's the program on now?"

"The Flintstones, of course."

"If I ever lived here, Matthew, you and I would have to work out some sort of an agreement about certain things."

"Well, you don't live here," Matthew said. "You just come over." He gave the shade such a hard yank that it rolled all the way up to the top of the window. Light glared into the room through the dirty naked glass.

"Oh shit!" I cried, sitting up. Matthew gave me a terrified glance and fled, slamming the door behind him. I got out of bed now to pull the shade down, dragging a chair over to the window so that I could stand on it to reach the cord. When I turned, Conrad was up too, already wearing his underpants, bending over the pile of clothes on the floor intent on separating his from mine.

I had the feeling he was on the run, as if he sensed he had inadvertently put himself into a weak position by referring casually to a subject he was careful never to discuss directly.

"I think I've lost a sock," he said. "Things seem to disappear in this house."

"No more than in any other."

I was angry with him for casting aspersions on my housekeeping, angry with him for being in such haste to leave. I found the sock under the radiator where the cats had dragged it, brushed the lint off it and held it out to him triumphantly. "*Voilà*," I said with bitterness.

"Thank you very much." He took it from me and sat down on the bed to put it on.

Although I knew it was the wrong moment to ask Conrad what I was going to ask, I also knew it was the only opportunity I was going to get. "Conrad, how about coming back here later?" It came out of me in a stiff and brittle tone that sounded more like an invitation to an argument than to a night of unbridled pleasure.

He stared at me, then asked me what I meant.

"I mean after you've done your work. I mean this evening."

He was silent. "You know I can't do that, Molly," he said with a weary patience.

"You could if you wanted to."

"I couldn't do that to Roberta."

"I don't give a fuck about Roberta," I said recklessly.

"I do."

"I know," I said.

"She's a human being, Molly, a very nice person. I treat her with the same respect I show to you."

"I'd say you treat her with more. Saturday nights are positively sacred to her."

"As it is," Conrad said, "she's upset that I can't be with her on Fridays."

"I would like to have two consecutive days with you, Conrad, just once. I would like to be with you on a weekend sometime."

"I understand your feelings." Conrad picked up his shirt and put his arms in the sleeves.

"What weekend could we spend together? Why don't you get out your little calendar?"

"How about Thursday and Friday two weeks from now. I'll be coming back from Chicago."

It took me only a second to assess the full meaning of what he'd said.

"She doesn't know a thing yet, does she?" I cried out wildly. "You've never told her anything? Where does she think you are the nights you spend with me?"

"I've given hints."

"*Hints!* You're bending over backwards to protect her

from knowing anything. Why do you protect her and not me?"

I asked the last question with a certain dread. I needn't have feared, however. Conrad was ready.

"Because she's a very fragile woman and you're a very self-sufficient one."

He finished buttoning his shirt and stood up to tuck it into his jeans. I watched him pull his zipper up and buckle his belt. He walked over to me and gave me a quick kiss. "I'll see you on Tuesday night," he said, "at seven. Unless you'd rather not."

"I would like to see you before then. I would like to see you tomorrow. You just arrange to get over here, Conrad!" I shouted as he walked to the bedroom door. He opened it, then turned for a moment.

"Your anger hurts me very much, Molly," he said sadly. "It seems to come from nowhere—especially after a beautiful night like the one we've just had."

It was after this that I began to be obsessed by the question of Roberta's lack of knowledge. It was this that came to assume an even larger place in my mind than Conrad's eventual separation from her. As Conrad would have been the first to say, no rational event occurs without a context.

Did Roberta know anything at all? Did she know nothing? Did she know—and choose not to know?

I had only what Conrad told me to guide me and my own intuition, which generally contradicted the impression he was trying to create. Roberta became fixed in my imagination in her unknowingness—which, like a magic garment, was both the potential source of her vulnerability and the secret of her curious power.

Conrad seemed frozen into his role as guardian of this enchanted state, unable to make even the first move that would unravel the situation. I wondered sometimes if he was someone who needed to be loved by as many people as possible, if he couldn't bear to let anyone go. I think he really did mean initially to let Roberta know by degrees that his affections had strayed to me; then when she seemed somewhat used to the idea, the break would occur. He was a man who would often be carelessly though never deliberately unkind. It could have been argued of course that the sooner Roberta knew, the kinder it would be in the end, the sooner her recovery would start.

I often asked myself what I would prefer in her position. I thought I would much rather know immediately, painful as it would be. I would suffer intensely for a time and then get on with my life. Although when I reflected upon the curious staying power I'd demonstrated during my marriage, I wasn't so sure of my own ability to cut loose from a hopeless situation. And I was even less sure when I asked myself how long I was going to give Conrad to work things out.

I longed for an accident that would reveal everything to Roberta—something quite out of Conrad's responsibility or control. As my obsession grew, I brooded upon possible ways in which knowledge could be communicated to her—scenarios like an encounter between the three of us in a crowded delicatessen, a chance meeting with her on Broadway as Conrad and I walked with our arms linked in a manner immediately suggesting intimacy. I rather dreaded the idea of such a confrontation, imagining her distress. And there was always the possibility that Conrad would rise to the occasion and introduce me as a client. And then there'd be the question of what I'd do.

I wanted to believe that I would boldly seize the opportunity to expose the truth—even at the risk of alienating Conrad temporarily. And yet I could also imagine myself standing there in silence, immobilized, as Rober-

70

ta's eyes searched our guilty faces, her voice shook as she said she was glad to meet me. It was as if we had exchanged places in the fantasies I used to have when I was married—wherein I tracked Fred down to the dark booth in Max's Kansas City where he was ensconced with his current twenty-two-year-old. I remember being quite aware that those long-limbed nymphs of Fred's owed me nothing. How could I expect them to defer to a marriage so obviously little valued? Nonetheless, I'd seen myself as a figure of wrath and grief, with justice on my side.

I had known about Fred of course. Without knowing the particulars, I had known and chosen to stay, however mistakenly. Despite Conrad's concern for her emotional well-being, Roberta, deprived of knowledge, was deprived of choice as well—and was thus in an intolerable position if she only knew it. As for me, I was in the consciously intolerable position of knowing all sides—or so I thought.

There is a corner bus stop on Seventy-second Street just after the Fifth Avenue bus makes the turn off Riverside Drive. She is sitting near the front of the bus with her child that Sunday. It is not quite noon and there are a number of empty seats behind them. She has been looking out of the window with only mild interest because the route is so familiar to her. A man and woman wait at the bus stop. The bus comes to a halt, the doors open to let them on. The woman is in her early twenties, tall and slender with short curly brown hair. She is dressed in perfectly fitting jeans with an expensive green suede jacket. She is laughing in a very animated way at something her escort has just said, tossing her curly head back, tilting her face upward toward his. She waits for him as he searches his pockets for change. The man with her is

71

Conrad, in a new navy blue turtleneck sweater that goes very well with his eyes. There is no doubt about it, they are a handsome couple.

"Look Mom, there's Conrad," Matthew says. "Hey Conrad! We're going to the zoo."

Conrad turns. His face stiffens slightly. Then he waves to Matthew with a big smile. By now he has found his change and he pays the fare. As he and the young woman pass the seat where she and Matthew are sitting, he pauses for a moment and says "Hello, Molly," in a voice that seems louder than necessary.

She is quite unable to answer. Turning away, she barely manages to nod. She can feel her left cheek, the one that is closest to the aisle, burning. No force on earth will make her look at him, will make her glance behind her as he and the young woman move on toward the rear and seat themselves about four rows back on the other side of the aisle.

Matthew is kneeling on his seat, intent on getting a better view of his old friend.

She tugs at the back of his belt. "Sit down, Matthew!"

"Mom, can I go and sit with Conrad?"

"No!"

She is trying to superimpose her image of Roberta upon the person she has just seen, although she knows it will not fit. It is not Roberta Conrad is with, but someone whose existence she has not even suspected. Perhaps Roberta herself does not exist in Conrad's life to the extent that she has been led to believe. She wonders how many different women there are. *How many, Conrad?* Is this the woman he sees on Sundays?

She is feeling dizzy. It is the close air, the slow, lurching movements of the bus. More people get on at Broadway, filling the empty seats, standing in the aisle next to her, above her. A stranger's belly presses against her shoulder. Finally she makes herself look behind her just once to where Conrad is absorbed in conversation with the other woman just as if she, Molly, is no more than any other passenger. His eyes wander in her direction for an instant, but it is not as though he sees her.

The bus stops at Lincoln Center and still more people pile on. They are all on top of each other, hanging from every strap. Where are they going? It is somehow indecent that they all must be contained like this in the same container—she and Conrad and . . .

The bus is moving forward again and she is suddenly standing, pulling on the cord, signalling she wants to get off. She grabs Matthew's hand and pushes through the bodies crowded near the front door, yanking him behind her. "But I thought we were going to the zoo!" he is wailing in rage and astonishment.

She doesn't have a plan. They will get there somehow, they will walk, take a taxi. They will end up going home. She cannot see herself looking at animals, at anything. "Excuse me," she is saying, "excuse me," breaking through to the door with her elbows, Matthew in tears as they exit.

"But I want to go to the zoo!"

They are standing on the pavement as the bus pulls away and she catches a glimpse of Conrad looking out at her behind glass, his red hair, his large stunned face.

It turns out later that she has jumped to conclusions again. The young woman she saw was "only Stephanie," a friend Conrad had neglected to mention to her—a former lover, but now more of a sister, a confidante. Some of his best friends are ex-lovers. He was upset by her conduct on the bus, her coldness. That was why he had not lingered or introduced Stephanie to her. "I think you have a propensity toward jealousy," he says. She has suffered for nothing.

73

* * *

I went to bed with my ex-husband on my birthday. Maybe because it was my birthday, maybe because it was another Saturday night that Conrad was spending with Roberta. Maybe because I was slightly depressed. Most of all, I suppose, I was curious. Who knows why you do certain dumb things? I do not discount curiosity as a factor. I was curious about what it would be like to go to bed with Fred when he was feeling attracted to me—and he *was* attracted now that he was past his initial territorial fury. Somehow the fact that I was desired by another had made me a desirable object in his eyes as well. At any rate, divorce clearly agreed with him. He came up to see Matthew that Saturday afternoon, took both of us out to dinner and resembled his old premarital self so much that I ended up sleeping with him accidentally, more by default than intention.

Later I asked myself whether we might have been making some unconscious effort toward reconciliation. But I don't think it was that. It was what it was—an act occurring in a sort of moral vacuum, to which it would be a mistake to ascribe too much meaning. Afterward we parted amicably, our mutual curiosity satisfied if nothing more. I didn't think to mention it to Conrad, since I was entitled to my own secrets. Not that I was hiding it, particularly. It just seemed to have very little to do with him—although I have little doubt in retrospect that it would not have occurred at all if our own relationship had been less tenuous.

It was an act, however, that had far-reaching repercussions. It was, in a sense, the accident I had been waiting for.

About ten days after my birthday, I woke up in the morning with severe pains in the lower part of my abdomen. I thought I had a virus—my diagnosis for all unspecific ailments. I would have stayed in bed if it had been a weekend, but it was a Monday and the proofs for the November issue of *New Thought* were coming in. I sent Matthew to school, took three aspirins and went to the office. I was sitting at my desk nearly doubled over with pain when the phone rang. It was Fred, yelling at me incoherently—something about "you and your goddamn fucking boyfriend."

"Fred, would you mind calming down and speaking a little more distinctly. I'm not feeling very well today."

I couldn't imagine why he was having an attack of jealousy at this late date, especially since we had not been in communication since the night he slept over. It was all much more than I was willing to deal with. My head throbbed and so did my belly. I felt close to tears.

"You got it from that rotten motherfucker and gave it to me!"

"Gave what, Fred?"

"The clap! Don't you even know what you're walking around with?"

"I'm not walking around with any such thing."

"I always thought you were a decent woman, Molly. We had our troubles, but I respected you. And now you're just going down the drain—going down the drain in every conceivable way. I'll never touch you again, you can be sure of that. We're finished, Molly. Finished."

I hung up. I sat at my desk a few moments, then got to my feet and painfully made my way to the cubicle of my friend Felicia, whom I consulted in all matters of catastrophe, both literary and personal. She was a diminutive, high-strung woman who had been book review editor of *New Thought* for fifteen years. During that time she had had three marriages, as well as numerous affairs with some of the best minds of her generation. Her glamorous but unsettled life and the physiological toll it had taken of her, her consuming interest in matters of the flesh, had made her an encyclopedia of valuable information about certain medical emergencies.

Felicia was on the phone when I approached her, the receiver cradled under chin while she made notes on the margins of a manuscript with her right hand and chain-smoked with her left. Always welcoming an opportunity for distraction, gossip or analysis of the personality traits of our colleagues, she smiled at me warmly, enthusiastically waving me to a chair piled high with books stuck with slips of paper. I sat down on the edge.

As my life once again tilted crazily, there was something reassuring about sitting here surrounded by so much familiar disorder—"creative chaos," Felicia called it. There was an odd comfort in the sight of the dusty proofs and manuscripts going back at least five years bulging precariously on the inadequate shelves, the back issues of journals piled high on the window sill next to the moribund philodendron, the emaciated avocado with its two surviving leaves. It was over this impressive accumulation that my friend reigned in perfect confidence that she alone knew where everything was.

As the conversation went on, Felicia made shrugs of resigned impatience, conveying to me by certain eloquent gestures that the person at the other end was outrageously boring and she couldn't wait to turn her full attention to me. "Logorrhea," she muttered, replacing the receiver in its cradle. "How are you, ducky?"

"I need to talk to you," I said portentously.

"Something wrong? Break up with Conrad, that bastard—although it might be all for the good? You don't look so well," she observed.

"I'm not well at all, Felicia."

"Oh my god. Not pregnant!"

I leaned toward her and said quietly, "I think I may have a social disease. Of all things. "

"Of all things indeed."

We both looked in alarm at the doorless entrance to the cubicle. Felicia rose from her desk, grabbed up her cigarettes. "Let's go into the ladies' room," she said in a low conspiratorial tone. Passing the accounting and subscription departments unobtrusively, we made our way there and locked ourselves in.

"Now tell me," Felicia said, flicking her ashes into the sink. "Do you think you have any definite symptoms?"

"Pain here," I said, pointing to my belly. "And I had a phone call from Fred."

"He gave it to you of course."

"He says I gave it to him."

"Nonsense. Or maybe not nonsense, considering the other one you're involved with. But more likely it's Fred. You know his habits."

"Yes," I said grimly.

"High promiscuity. I'd say he's been asking for it. And now he's just trying to displace the blame. Very nice." Felicia scowled.

"I'm just feeling a little overwhelmed," I said. "I've never experienced anything like this."

"I have. And various other forms of sexual punishment. Of course you're overwhelmed. And just when you're getting settled in your new apartment."

"I could have lived without it."

"Of course, ducky." Despite my possibly diseased condition, Felicia put her arm around me and gave me an affectionate squeeze. "Take my advice and go right away—right this minute—to the public health clinic on Twenty-fourth Street. According to the *New York Times*, they've been handling up to three hundred cases a day."

"As many as that!"

"It's reaching epidemic proportions. Don't you read the papers?"

I confessed with some embarrassment that I usually skipped the medical news.

"Not allergic to penicillin, are you?" I shook my head. "Then you should have absolutely no problem. Of course, there is a particular strain from Indochina that's highly resistant to penicillin and for which there's no known cure. But I think it's quite unlikely you've contracted that. Want me to come with you?" she asked kindly. "I'll cancel my lunch date."

An offer of support was something I had encountered so rarely that I was thrown into confusion, not knowing

78

whether to accept it or to decline. "No," I said, "I think I'll be all right."

I took a taxi only as far as Twenty-second Street and got out in front of a moving and storage company. I walked the rest of the way. A school stood next to my destination. Cutouts of autumn leaves and jack o' lanterns were pasted against its windows and there were the innocent cries of first-graders from the playground.

The lobby of the Public Health Clinic smelled of disinfectant, just as I had anticipated. A pimp in high-heeled silver shoes walked briskly past me. A guard, snapping his fingers to a transistor radio, stood behind a little table.

I walked up to him.

"Which way to the social disease department?" I asked.

He looked me up and down. "Uh *huh*," he said with a grin. He pointed left.

The waiting room of the women's section of the social disease department was totally lacking in amenities. Not one copy of the *Ladies' Home Journal,* not one picture of fruit and flowers on its institutional-green walls, not one potted plant. It was thronged with patients waiting on the hard plastic benches—women of every age and description.

Distracting myself from the business at hand by pretending I was more a sociologist than a patient, I studied my fellow afflicted—the tense young student in the corner biting her lips as she bent over her French grammar; the grandmotherly woman with Clairol-red hair, stolidly crocheting; the model in pants suit with perfectly matched accessories; the weary mother anxiously keeping track of the three small children who accompanied her—and across the room from me, clinging to each other in a highly wrought-up state, two young women I recognized from the few times Fred had taken me to Max's Kansas City, who had been described to me as "making all the parties," as well as being frequently written up in the "scenes" column of the *Village Voice*. In the fluorescent light of the clinic, they looked like two bedraggled night birds, their vintage patchwork finery fluttering limply around their bare skinny thighs, their drugged, painted eyes wide with apprehension as they awaited the results of their tests.

The disease, I reflected, was a great equalizer, cutting across all distinctions of class. (I was sure Conrad would be interested in that particular observation.) It was entirely possible one could sit next to a perfect stranger who had been a crucial link in the chain of one's own infection.

Perhaps unjustly, I studied the girls from Max's with special interest, making certain speculations as to their circle of acquaintanceship. One of them glanced across the room at me with a bemused look that indicated I might have seemed somewhat familiar—but where . . . ? She looked away again quickly, desiring eye contact as little as I did. I took out some proofs I'd brought with me and listened for my name.

It is her ability to create distance that carries her through many a trying situation. In her twenties, she had worried, even anguished over this tendency to absent the Me at various crucial moments—thus possibly denying herself the full range of human experience. Now she suspects that certain varieties of experience are simply not worth having.

Where is the value in this present one, for example?

The recognition of the extent of the insidious corruption whose outward manifestation is this spreading disease that is nothing if not social?

Conrad often criticizes her for leading an all too privatized existence, for living somewhat aloof from the great social movements of her time. Now she is caught up against her will in this one—and so, by implication, is he.

"Would you mind letting us have a list of your contacts?" the special investigator asks (after she has been examined, pronounced positive and dosed with penicillin). He indicates to her the appropriate spaces on the yellow form where names are to be filled in. He is an ordinary bland young man who could just as well have become an insurance agent or a bank teller. She wonders what quirk of fate has led him into this unusual branch of the Civil Service.

For a moment she hesitates, confronting the moral issue raised by this unexpected extension of the honor system.

"I have no contacts," she lies—which the young investigator accepts in perfect faith, since the fact that the disease has in a sense come to her honestly, through her husband, indicates a certain respectability.

He even blushes a little, explaining that this is just a routine question, since it is the practice of the department to follow up all leads relating to contacts, notifying same to report for immediate examination and treatment.

"Of course," she says pleasantly, handing the form with its unfilled spaces back to him. She knows instinctively that countless others have automatically committed this identical act of civil disobedience. No wonder the disease has flourished. There are areas in human

81

affairs from which the state must be excluded at all costs.

She will have to tell Conrad herself as soon as possible. And he will then have to tell Roberta. And suddenly she sees the disease in a new light entirely. It is a form of communication!

When I've been injured by someone close to me, I am astonished at first, almost paralyzed. And then I become more and more troubled by whatever is incomprehensible—the opaque and brittle crust that forms over an act, concealing motives, reasons, without which the act itself appears gratuitous, even irrational. I pick away at this crust as if at one of the scabs ever present on my knees during childhood—a bit of it flakes off and then more and I almost stop, anticipating the pain that will be like the ghost of the original wound. And yet I'm drawn to continue to the end, to reveal the contours of whatever lies beneath.

Conrad was not like me. He often made the mistake of interpreting my questioning as vengefulness—not understanding that it was more my wish to gather facts than to sit in judgment upon them. It was a subtle game he played—he the embodiment of good nature, I the embodiment of suspicion and anxiety. His own good nature was certainly his most outstanding feature, shining forth even in the most inappropriate circumstances. Who knew what dark thoughts lurked in the mind of the Great Accepter?

Here, for example, was how he greeted the news of my infidelity and its unfortunate consequences when I saw him that Tuesday evening.

"I'm not going to ask you to explain, Molly. Under the circumstances, I hardly have the right."

All of this was uttered in the mildest tones. He might have been inquiring why his shirt had not gone to the laundry. I felt abashed in the face of so much generosity. Another man might have indulged in recriminations. I wondered why he felt he didn't have the right.

"I am a little surprised, though," he admitted. "I know you weren't considering going back to Fred."

"Will it make any sense if I tell you I honestly don't know why I did it?"

"Why should I expect things to make sense? I just wish you'd picked a better time for your reunion." He grinned philosophically.

I turned away from him and stared at the rug.

I had spent two days in dread of this meeting—preparing to deal with Conrad's jealousy and rage, to confront him openly even at the risk of being thrust away. As soon as I'd come back from the clinic, I'd called his office. His secretary thought he'd gone away for the weekend and had not yet returned to the city. Intermittently I tried his apartment. In the evening my sense of responsibility drove me to consider leaving a note under his door. But what could I have written?

Feeling a confusing bitterness, I waited for my guilt to return.

84

"Well, I guess I'll go to the clinic tomorrow," Conrad said. "Where did you say it was?"

"Twenty-forth Street."

"I wonder how early they open. I'll have to go before the office. Dammit, I have a ten o'clock appointment."

"I'm really sorry about this, Conrad," I said.

"There's absolutely no room in my schedule for getting sick. But who knows?" he reflected cheerfully. "Maybe I don't even have it. I haven't felt any symptoms. What is it for men—a sort of burning sensation?"

"I guess it's still just incubating."

Conrad frowned. "Let's see. You saw Fred on a Saturday?"

"It was my birthday."

He ignored the implication. "And when was it we got together after that?"

"Last Tuesday."

"That's four days' difference . . . "

"Maybe you'll get the shot soon enough so you won't come down with it in a bad way."

"That would be good." But he was sounding much less optimistic. An anxious look had become visible on his face.

"I really did keep trying to get in touch with you before this."

"I was around," he said vaguely.

"I even left messages at your office. I suppose I could have reached you last night, but naturally I didn't try."

"Where would you have reached me?"

"At Roberta's. I didn't think you'd appreciate it much."

"It would not have been a good idea."

"I could have pretended to be someone else. I could even have pretended to be me, since she doesn't know who I am anyway." Somehow, even in this situation, I

85

ended up as the injured one. Inevitably all our quarrels led to the same place.

"Oh come on, Molly!"

"Suppose there ever really was a bad emergency. Could I reach you there?"

"Of course you could," he said.

"Conrad, you really are the limit!"

"Well, in a *genuine emergency* of course—"

"But it would have to be a matter of life and death. Not something as trivial as this. Even though in this case it affects her too." This is not the way, not the way, I told myself—attempting to no avail to hold myself in check.

"It really does affect her, Conrad."

"I'm aware of that," he said grimly.

"You're going to have to tell her."

"I had no thought of doing otherwise."

"Maybe it's even for the best. You never know."

"How do you figure that?"

"Well, nothing's ever as bad as whatever it is you dread. Even the clap is just something you cure right away with penicillin. Nobody dies of it. I'm feeling much better since I got my shot."

Enacting a tenderness I did not exactly feel, I touched his hair, ran my hand down his impassive cheek.

We had been sitting next to each other all this time on the living-room couch and now abruptly he stood up. "I think I should go," he said.

"You're not going to stay over?"

"Not tonight, Molly. Not tonight."

Separated by the expanse of the coffee table, they are sitting on their injections in her living room listening to Mahler's First Symphony—which Conrad has turned up to full volume, making conversation nearly impossible. It is a lack in her that she is not particularly fond of Mahler herself. She would have picked something by Satie for this occasion, or perhaps the Billy Holliday recording of "Don't Explain." In any case, she knows that in other more important ways, too, they are out of tune with each other. It is the beginning of a new and more difficult period. Tonight she is irritated by the way she has seen him listen to music so often before—eyes half closed, fingers swaying an imaginary baton. If not for his fascination with the law, his dedication to social justice, he might have become a world-famous conductor or at least a fiddler in the Philharmonic. How intensely he appreciates Mahler's genius—shutting her out. She remembers the interminable Saturday afternoons of her childhood when there was no one to play with and her parents were listening to the opera.

It is raining outside, a cold late October downpour that floods the rear courtyard below, setting the garbage can lids afloat. Full of Mahler-gloom, she gets up and stands at the window, staring into a brilliantly lit apartment across the way where a pimp and his two women are smoking grass, passing a communal joint ceremoniously from hand to hand, sometimes stopping to toss a ball to their small communal poodle. She thinks for some reason of some lines of Pound's that she has not read for a long time:

> *And I am happier than you are,*
> *And they were happier than I am;*
> *And the fish swim in the lake and do not even own*
>   *clothing.*

She is nearly overwhelmed by the poignancy, the irony, of the last line. "And the fish swim in the lake . . ." One of the women, a tall, spectacular blonde in little satin hot-pants, comes to the window and stares aggressively into the night. Perhaps she sees Molly standing at her own window. The front paws and head of the poodle appear beside her. The woman pulls a cord and draws the drapes, which are of some heavy dull golden silk, probably synthetic. A pinkish light glows behind them for a few moments and then goes out.

She turns and finds Conrad watching her—not warmly but with a kind of guarded objectivity, the way one might watch an attractive but unpredictable wild animal from a distance as one wonders what it will conceivably do next.

He never mentioned Roberta. It was as if I had dropped a pebble into a pool and it had sunk straight to the bottom without a trace of that expected pattern of concentric spreading rings. Now I was left on the shore staring at the smooth surface of the water which gave me back only my own reflection.

I didn't mention her either. Things were much too fragile for that.

Some people can never admit to being angry. They will sit in stony silence, they will pretend to be affable, they will engage in meaningless civilities, they will physically remove themselves from the premises if they have to— anything but reveal that they are gripped by strong emotion.

Conrad seemed determined not to react except obliquely. He continued to come around to see me the same two nights of the week just as if nothing had happened. There was no repetition of the time he had fled. His references to his experiences in the clinic, to the discomfort he was prepared to gallantly and stoically endure as the price of our association, were wryly humorous. He drank the tea I made for him in lieu of the wine that was forbidden, but impatiently dismissed any other ministering efforts on my part—as if in some way they might mock him. He wasn't quite sure of me now that I had become the transgressor and he the victim.

There was no doubt that I had inflicted a wound upon him where he was most vulnerable—the locus of his pride and anxiety, that bit of flesh he employed with such wonderful dexterity, that unfailing flesh that imperiously ruled him, that was in a sense his Achilles' heel. He concealed it from me, on the nights when we retired together, under a layer of stretched white cotton—as if even my gaze might contaminate it further. Not wishing to be naked where he was not, I took to undressing in the bathroom and covering myself with my flannel nightgown. We would sleep with a cold breadth of sheet between us—although we might have held each other, there would have been no harm in that. Nothing but affection would have been transmitted by our kisses.

In the past we had invariably reached temporary settlements of our differences in bed—there was always that attraction that seemed to have a life of its own, so that even in the midst of the most profound verbal rift, there was the implicit knowledge that shortly we would be physically joined. But now the pleasure that had initially caused our fall from grace was denied to us just when we needed it to fall back on.

It was small consolation to me that in my ex-husband's eyes, at least, I was vindicated. He eventually called me and confessed with some embarrassment that he'd totally forgotten a passing encounter with a certain young lady from an East Side discotheque a few nights before we slept together. She had since left for Paris with a rock group, so there had been no way of verifying his suspicions, but still it seemed to him now that she must have been the source, and he was glad because he would not have wanted to have thought of me without respect, since after all he had been joined in wedlock to me and I would always be the mother of his child, that fine little guy whom he intended to see every other Sunday if he could manage it. He humbly hoped that I had not been seriously inconvenienced, etc. It was one of Fred's finest moments. He had never been a man given to making apologies. Perhaps the shifting fortunes he'd experienced recently had begun to have a humanizing effect.

I told him I had no hard feelings. "Well, live and let live," I said. It costs nothing to be forgiving when one no longer loves.

And yet if Fred had been seeking vengeance, he could not have chosen a more effective form.

I think Conrad was always a little afraid of me after that. The anger he never expressed remained with him, a secret hidden even from his conscious self. I am guessing, of course. Certainly his behavior was entirely in keeping with his ideology. If he believed in perfect freedom for himself, how could he deny the same freedom to a woman without being sexist? Roberta, I suppose, was as free in his mind as I was. And since she and I and he were all equally free, we all could do as we pleased in respect to each other. From a theoretical standpoint it worked perfectly. Fred, needless to say, never thought about such questions at all. And I am not sure myself that emotions are subject to theory.

Even in Conrad's realm of theoretical freedom, there were boundaries as well as a definite hierarchy. Conrad was on top, of course. Just below him there was Roberta and sometimes me—our positions kept fluctuating. There were times when she was what he called "the primary re-

90

lationship" and times when I was. Or maybe I never was more than secondary. I *felt* primary in the beginning—if one can trust one's feelings. Later I felt entitled-to-be-primary—which is not quite the same. Let me see if I can define "primary relationship." It is the one that is considered the objective rather than the obstacle to the objective. It is the one that is to be worked out in the future, the obstacle having been dealt with and laid to rest. It is the one that is rational, that is consciously chosen, the secondary being considered a neurotic attachment.

What I had lost forever in Conrad's eyes, I think, was the peculiarly virginal status of a woman just liberated from marriage. Conrad would be the first to disagree with me on this point, since virgins have no place at all in his theoretical system. An encounter with a real virgin and the responsibilities thereof would almost be too much for him—and I think he would wisely abstain. However, the virgin, rare as she has come to be in our culture above a certain age group, still occupies an exalted place in the hearts of men, still is highly prized, is in fact the ultimate possession, the fulfillment of that masculine desire to go where no man has gone before. I cannot believe that Conrad was that different from men in general, that the mask of the libertarian did not conceal the stern visage of the puritan. How else to explain his consistent passion for the newly separated—Roberta, for example, and then me, and I can recall hearing him speak of other women in that condition with an unmistakable flickering of erotic interest. Was it merely coincidence, was it really nothing more than his attraction to someone's particular qualities in each case? Was it not that we were all as close as he could come to the real thing, women just out of the convent, our innocence restored by years of separation from the world of casually traded sex, ready for his imprinting.

Conrad, I am being hard on you. I am not acknowledging your specialness. I am only drawing conclusions from what I have observed—the inevitable rush of masculine attention when a married woman first "comes out." Later it markedly drops away. Who can explain it?

I allowed myself to be deflowered. I dragged you into the mud, Conrad. I lost my aura, became less for you. I am sorry.

Roberta was clearly primary after all that. I receded, dropped to second place.

I wonder what he told her. He told her something, but I am almost certain it was not the truth. Since she was given, according to Conrad, to *Sturm und Drang*, I imagine she wept and stormed and reduced him to humiliation. Then, when all seemed most hopeless, perhaps there was a touching scene of forgiveness—no less effective for the fact that she probably knew she was going to forgive him all along.

I finally did ask Conrad what happened.

"By the way, what happened with Roberta?"

"She took it in her stride."

Thanksgiving was going to be bad that year. I could feel it approaching like a doom by the second week of November, when exhortations went up in supermarket windows to ORDER YOUR TURKEY NOW. Conrad was going to spend it with his mother. I had never met that particular lady of mythic needs. "Why don't I make dinner for all of us?" I suggested in a casual tone. "I really wouldn't mind."

Conrad looked somewhat startled. "No Molly, it's nice of you, but it wouldn't work out. I don't think she'd understand."

I'd actually had a mad and hopeful vision for a moment of all of us around the dinner table together, a kind of false family—Conrad's mother naturally being somewhat reserved in her feelings toward me as I dished out the turkey (hopefully not too dry), the chestnut stuffing (which she would probably find too heavy) and the spicy cranberry relish (which she would no doubt refuse), but since she was said to be very fond of small male children, she was sure to be enchanted at any rate by Matthew, who would have to submit to a bath, shampoo and clean-up of his room for the occasion. Conrad, never a picky eater, would have seconds and thirds of everything and come back during the week to finish up the leftovers.

"What's there to understand?" I said.

Silence. An embarrassed look.

"Well, I'm not much in the mood for Thanksgiving anyway. If it wasn't for Matthew, I wouldn't make any kind of fuss at all, just eat spaghetti or something or go out to a Chinese restaurant and have Peking Duck."

"Now, there's a good idea," Conrad said cheerfully.

"Maybe that's what I'll do."

I sat very still for a moment. "Excuse me," I said. I got up and went and locked myself in the bathroom. I cried for several minutes, turning the cold water on so that it rushed loudly into the sink and splashing it all over my face before I came out.

"You look funny," Conrad said.

"Do I?"

"Flushed."

I turned my face away from him. He put his hand on my chin and turned it around again. "Is something wrong?"

"No."

"You've been crying."

"It's just my annual pre-holiday depression. It's a little bit worse this year."

"I always have dinner with my mother."

"It's all right. Really. At my age I should be immune to the holidays."

94

"I am," Conrad said with satisfaction. "Quite immune."

"Maybe you could come over afterwards."

"I'd like to very much, but it might be too late. I'll try to call you." I wondered whether he spent Christmas with his mother, too. What about New Year's? But he was looking at me so kindly now, so warmly. It had been a long time since such warmth had emanated from him. I put my arms around Conrad, burrowed my face into his shoulder and sobbed almost contentedly. I felt him knead the back of my neck; his other hand moved firmly and gently down my thigh, cupped my knee.

"I know a wonderful cure for depression," he whispered.

Such cures are momentary, and may be more distracting than curative. My depression returned full force the next morning, as did the problem of how to survive Thanksgiving, since Conrad had not succeeded in imparting any of his immunity. It might even be said that his own was debatable, since as far as I know he participated fully in the celebration of every family holiday during the time that I knew him—though never with me. One can only assume, I suppose, a profound attitude of alienation on his part in the very midst of the festivities.

I am certainly still in total agreement with him that the emotionally laden American Holiday Season has deteriorated into little more than a capitalist potlatch based upon the appallingly dishonest assumption that everybody in this basically fragmented and troubled society either is or should suddenly be feeling terrific for at least a month.

I could do without the whole damn period myself except for the long weekends. It embarrasses me considerably that just as if I am no older than Matthew, I feel it is my due to be happy on certain days of the year—and that I am therefore particularly unhappy in the knowledge that I will be feeling as rotten, as shut out in the cold as the Little Match Girl. On the chilly dawn of Christmas morning, I will be alone in my empty bed trying to assemble the G.I. Joe helicopter that is the heart's desire of my child, tears running out of my eyes and curses streaming from my lips as I struggle with the brittle plastic parts that will not snap together. On Thanksgiving it's always the Macy's Parade and having to stand among all the families—the mommies and daddies, stepfathers and lovers—shivering in the November cold on Central Park West, awaiting the ancient, patched balloons that floated through my own childhood. And I grip Matthew's little hand that is like a soft anchor, because I don't like to stand there manless, childless. But of course I let him pull away from me. For isn't he entitled to crawl under the police barrier to the curb, to see everything, to talk to the clowns?

"I assume, naturally," Felicia said, appearing suddenly one morning in the entrance to my cubicle at the office, "that you are otherwise engaged—but in case you aren't, I've decided to have a few friends come over on Thanksgiving. I detest turkey, so I'm making a goose. There's an excellent recipe in Julia Child, much better than the one in *Larousse Gastronomique*. I don't know whether you've ever tried it."

"No I haven't." I was staring at her with astonished gratitude. "I'd love to come," I said. "I am not otherwise engaged."

Felicia sighed. "I somehow thought you might not be.

You must bring Matthew," she said. "I adore that child, that intelligent, wonderful face."

"Can I bring anything else?"

"Spinach greens. Five pounds. Snip off the stems and give them three rinsings to get out the sediment. But maybe you don't really want to wash all that spinach— it's an onerous task at best."

"I don't mind at all. Felicia, I feel rescued."

"That's what we all must do. We must rescue ourselves and others. Well, I'm delighted you're coming and I assure you you won't find it dull. It's going to be entirely a gathering of women."

A gathering of women. I remember the defiant elegance of the menu. It was pumpkin soup that we started with. "It should have been a pie, Felicia!" Matthew said sternly. He was too young to accept such reversals. The grownups had had more practice— having experienced not only the transformations of pumpkins into the unexpected but desire into distaste, marriage into divorce, parenthood into custody, love into separation. Farther uptown or downtown, east or west, the ears of the uninvited absent burned perhaps, or perhaps not, in the consoling presences of other women—yes, they had all probably found new women by now. There was an oversupply of women, a surplus. The sadistic husband of forty-four could find an eager girl of twenty-two. The alcoholic could find sympathy. The relentless bore was in demand for mixed dinners.

On and on the women talked, getting quite loud sometimes, each eager to succeed the next, hold the floor for a moment with tales of even more outrageous atrocities suffered and survived. I contributed reminiscences of my marriage, warming up with the chicken pox episode and

97

going on to a spirited description of the summer Fred had rented a bungalow without indoor plumbing on the Jersey Shore for me and Matthew to go away to every weekend so that he could have an affair with someone in our air-conditioned apartment.

One strikingly attractive woman whose psychiatrist husband had always mercilessly criticized her appearance, her cooking, her lack of interest in current affairs, her inability to balance the checking account and to be gay at cocktail parties, now offered him up to the other assembled guests, as if on auction. Gray and distinguished, she said, good tennis player, lucrative practice. Jolly, she said, though we all looked at her dubiously. Yes, jolly. "Very ho ho ho," she said, holding her rounded arms in front of her as if to indicate a Santa Claus-shaped figure. "Any takers?"

There were none, of course. In this context we all had the highest standards. At least Conrad was not critical, I thought. The woman who'd had the psychiatrist husband also had a lover now—someone much younger than she was who adored her. She admitted she lived in so much terror the affair would end, she could not allow herself to be happy.

We laughed with her at that paradox. More wine was passed around. Matthew wandered away from the table and turned on the television, where an impoverished family of eight during the depression had just won a turkey on a church raffle ticket bought by the thirteen-year-old daughter who was dying of leukemia. He lay on the rug dreamily eating a cupcake with orange frosting that had been specially purchased for him. It was way past his bedtime. He had no interest in the soufflé Grand Marnier that had now been brought in from the kitchen. By the time the commercial came on, he was asleep. I tiptoed across the room and turned off the set, the women's voices, the laughter, rising now to an even higher pitch over the extravagant sweetness, the seductive texture of the dessert, the forbidden caloric pleasure. Felicia, released finally from culinary responsibility, was holding forth, quoting a line from Hemingway: "If a woman is good, she doesn't need a pillow." "Oh that's too wonderful, he couldn't have written that," someone said. But it appeared that he had, it was somewhere in *For Whom the Bell Tolls*, and the rest of us wondered how we had ever missed it. But the point of mentioning it at all, Felicia said, the important point was the seriousness with which she, intellectually and sexually precocious at fifteen, had originally taken it, having only the vaguest idea of its meaning. "I was quite determined that (a) I was going to be good and (b) I was never going to need a pillow." "And have you?" the woman who had been married to the jolly psychiatrist called out. "Never," she responded grandly. "Never in thirty years."

I laughed with the others until my throat ached and my eyes smarted. But I was suddenly anxious. It was nearly eleven and what if Conrad was trying to reach me? Any minute now he might be saying good night to his mother, going to the phone—even though he hadn't promised. He'd only said he'd try.

I ended up being the first one to leave, shamelessly rushing away from there toward the arms of the enemy, refusing cognac and coffee, using Matthew as an excuse—the child needed his sleep—although everyone could see he was sleeping very comfortably. He cried when I woke him to put on his shoes and jacket—I struggled fiercely with the zipper of the latter which always stuck just when you were in a hurry—besides which, it is very hard to zip another person. "Goddamn crumby zipper," I said, because it was late, it was late, I was losing valuable seconds. The phone rang insistently in my mind. Felicia gave Matthew a kiss and a fistful of nuts and we descended into the dark and empty street and I hailed a cab. We were home by eleven-fifteen. And then I sat up for the next two hours and waited.

I used to do that very often, Conrad—rush away from somewhere because I thought you might be going to call me. Who knows what I missed on those truncated evenings of my life? Once I was at a delightful party engaged in an intense and promising conversation with an immensely attractive man I'd just met. I walked away from him in the middle of a sentence—and you didn't call that night, after all. You were never tied to me like that—*wired* would be more accurate—wired to me with invisible telephone wire. I thought I could actually feel the calls trying to come through sometimes, getting short-circuited—although the line was always open.

Felicia once told me she'd had a special phone installed with a number known only to her lover, so that he could always reach her, even at the very moment she was talking to someone else on the other phone. Although it would have embarrassed me to have gone that far for anyone, I admired her ingenuity. It was only a small additional charge on her bill and for her it was a solution. I understood her anxiety perfectly. He used it three or four times, I think, and then they broke up. Maybe it was too much for him—the significance of such unabashed availability. Never personally having been on the other end of it, I cannot imagine what it would be like.

Conrad was not even in town that Thanksgiving or for the rest of that weekend, as it turned out. He was in Philadelphia with Roberta and her family.

BAD CONNECTIONS

It was Deborah who told me. Perceiving me clearly on this occasion as the underdog, the victim, she broke silence at last and phoned to tell me of running into Roberta at the exercise class earlier that week. She described to me Roberta's joy and self-congratulatory sense of accomplishment—Conrad had been so difficult recently, so moody and unpredictable, but now it seemed, under the ascendancy of her influence, he was straightening out.

She has taken to her bed, hiding out there under the covers, burning up one minute, cold the next—pretending for Matthew's benefit that she is ill with something real. But the pain is real enough, although the illness is not. She gives him extensive direction on how to make himself a peanut butter sandwich and sinks back against the pillows exhausted, knowing she should be marketing, taking out the laundry. But her whole head is burning, her cheeks are aflame; the fire rises up all the way to her scalp, travels along her hair, singeing it at the edges. She is a person who has been lied to, casually humored then betrayed.

"I have a headache too, Mom." Matthew's small body plumps down next to her on the bed companionably.

"No you haven't, Matthew."

"Yes I do. I need a baby aspirin."

"You're acting like a baby."

103

JOYCE JOHNSON

He thinks it over. "Maybe," he says.

She hears a shrill, unpleasant voice obviously belonging to someone at the end of her tether cry out, "For god's sake! Will you leave me alone!" He lies there quite still, unnaturally solemn. Striken by guilt, she explains that this desire characteristic of grownups is often hard for children to understand. She asks him if he would please just take her word for it.

Recovering immediately, he argues that this is not necessarily true of children because he, Matthew, understands everything she tells him.

"In that case, would you please go and play in your room for a while."

He goes away for fifteen minutes, during which she cries and wonders whether in addition to everything else she is turning into a rotten mother—hating Conrad for that, too. Hating him. Yes, that is certainly the emotion she feels and she wants only to tell him that immediately, reach him immediately with the clean, fresh hatred pure and undissipated. *That is what I want to do,* she thinks with one half of her, the other half in anguish thinking that she has lost him, lost him without knowing it because he didn't even have the guts to tell her. All the time he was sitting on her couch looking at her in that concerned way, taking her in his arms, he knew damn well what he was really going to be doing this weekend—not to mention all the obvious connotations of that trip out of town with Roberta. What could that mean except what she thought it did—that formality of going to meet the parents?

And she never even knew it, never suspected—all these weeks everything going on as usual, except for the strain between them for a while, and even that had disappeared. And that is somehow the worst of it—the knife that twists again and again—that she hadn't known, that she has been just as unconscious as she ever thought Roberta was. They have each known different portions of the truth—and in the gap between Conrad swims back and forth with the untroubled ease of a fish, back and forth from one to the other. So that even now if by all the external evidence she thinks she has lost him, that too may be an appearance, nothing more than that, just something she was not supposed to ever find out. He will appear on Tuesday just as usual. "Did you have a good Thanksgiving?" he will ask.

"Hello. I don't think you know me. But I know who you are."

I finally settled on that as my opening. If I could just say that much, get that far, I could say the rest—having rejected "We met a couple of years ago in Amagansett, but I don't think you would remember me," as too much like normal conversation. It was conceivable that, losing nerve, one might go on from there to a discussion of summer houses in Amagansett, mutual friends and other trivia and never get to the point. In "I know who you are" there was a certain undertone of dark suggestion, committing one irrevocably to what was to follow.

It was not that I wanted to frighten Roberta—it was that I distrusted myself. I was afraid of leaving too much room for my cowardice or my scruples—I wasn't sure which might serve to inhibit me. Last minute cowardice probably. There was an unspoken but very strong taboo against certain acts of communication between women—a taboo undoubtedly first invented by men, protecting their sacred prerogative to pick and choose and sample, all in the estimable cause of "finding themselves." God forbid! What if they didn't! And yet taboos are made

105

to be broken. There are acts almost inconceivable in contemplation that in execution are as simple as picking up a phone and dialing the seven digits of a particular number. The phone rings. One holds on to the receiver, heart beating, and waits. "Hello. I don't think you know me . . ." Anyone could say it. Who says that a woman cannot talk to another woman?

The more I thought about making that call during that long and bitter weekend, the more it seemed the only thing to do—if not the right thing. Seen from a distance, the act had a cold and shining hardness about it, drawing me on toward the moment of commission with the silent force of a magnet. And yet could I really do it? Could I become transformed from the depressed and essentially forgiving person I thought I was into someone quite unfamiliar—a sort of terrorist striking with a flaming Biblical sword? *I think it is only fair that you should know the truth, Roberta.*

Oh, I was determined to be fair. She was not, after all, my enemy. The real enemy was Conrad's indecision. We were both its victims—although she was a victim more privileged than I, occupying a larger and more comfortable cell. I wondered if even in Philadelphia, at her parents' table, she felt really sure of him—if even there she felt a persistent uncertainty, the sense of inexplicable omissions just below the surface, days and nights unaccounted for, secret transgressions, inconsistencies. Had he promised her he was turning over a new leaf? She would have believed it, of course, just as I would have believed that kind of promise myself—because I wanted to. Conrad himself might even believe it, temporarily. He would come to see me with a reserved and solemn face— "Molly, I have something to tell you . . ."

106

I turned and twisted in my unmade bed. I staggered to the kitchen and heated a can of soup, ladled it into a bowl and ended by pouring it into the sink, clogging the drain with noodles. If I had lost him anyway, there was nothing left to lose. I could make the call or not, it wouldn't matter. I would know only the satisfaction of acting rather than being acted upon. Did the means then justify themselves?

I reached for the kitchen phone and dialed his number—not hers—giving him his last chance to explain, to tell me what was going to happen in my life. I wanted to hear it all now, not Tuesday. How could I wait another three days or even another hour? I almost hoped he would lie to me. That would be a sign he still cared enough to try to keep me. But I would have to be hard on him, tell him what I knew, not allow him to deny it. Holding the receiver slightly away from my ear, I listened to the phone ring eight times. He always picked it up by the third ring if he was home. But it was not yet the end of the weekend, it was only Saturday night. They were still together, unreachable in some private space sacred to couples, "out of town for the holidays" like any more conventional pair, taking a respite from the pressures of the city. No need to hasten their return.

They came back on Sunday. Around eight there was a busy signal on Conrad's line. Perhaps at that moment he was trying to reach me. I never asked him. After I hung up, I picked up the phone and dialed again. By this time I knew the other number by heart.

"Hello," she said in the flat, little girl's voice that I remembered.

"Hello. Is this Roberta?" I recognized the crisp, civil

tone as the one I used in the office when talking to strangers.

"Yes?"

"My name is Molly Held. I know who you are but you don't know me." I realized after I had spoken that I had reversed the order of my original statement, given it a baldness, a bluntness, it had not had before.

"Am I supposed to?" she asked rather coldly.

"No. We are not—either of us—supposed to know each other. I'm calling because I felt there was something you ought to be aware of."

"And what is that?" she asked after a moment.

"I am a person whom Conrad has been seeing. He has been seeing me rather seriously for several months now."

There was a silence.

"I suppose he never mentioned it. I thought he would have told you himself. Anyway, I'm tired of being the person who knows everything. We both should know all sides."

"Look," she said, "I don't understand how Conrad could be seeing you. He's with me every night of the week."

I had to ponder the logic of what she had just told me. I wondered—if it was true that I could not be seen—whether I existed, whether Conrad existed. "Well," I said clumsily, all my adroitness, my desire to maintain a certain delicacy, having deserted me, "someone must be lying. Why don't you think about it? Goodbye," I said and hung up.

Felicia, whose wisdom about the nuances of human relationships I trust absolutely, has often warned me about the unreliability of dialogues imagined in advance of their occurrence—a lesson learned through her own tendency to endlessly project and rehearse, taking both parts—her own and that of her adversary. "It always comes out very differently from what you expected, Molly. That's the only certainty you can count on."

I think I had expected anything but a denial. Hurt, certainly. Rage—directed against Conrad rather than at me, although I might have borne the brunt of it at first. But finally she would have recognized the essential morality of what I had done. The bringer of the truth is always in the right.

I believed that then, but since I've come to question it. Was I not also punishing Roberta in deliberately depriving her of her illusion of happiness—the truth then being not merely itself, gratuitously delivered, but the instrument of a less admirable motive? I did not want her to be happier than I was, even if that happiness was based upon a deception and therefore not objectively real. I wanted her to suffer as I was suffering, and only in that sharing was I prepared to be generous, fantasizing a commiseration that Conrad would have abhorred between two women who had so much in common.

He called me about twenty minutes later. "Are you expecting to be in for a while, Molly?"

"As far as I know."

"I'd like to come over to talk to you."

"Do as you please, Conrad!" I shouted. "Do as you please!"

"I'm coming over." There was a click.

How dare he ask if I was going to be in? Wasn't I almost always in, there at his convenience? Didn't he always know just exactly where I was? But that was going to change, I thought wildly, that was going to change. Tomorrow I was going to start a whole new life, become a person who went out a lot. Energized by rage, I whirled through the apartment, straightening, tidying, sweeping the accumulated mess of the weekend into corners and drawers—a rampage of order. "Get your things out of the living room!" I yelled to Matthew, locking myself into the bathroom to strip off the nightgown I had worn for two days and change into sweater and jeans, brush my hair—my hands shaking as I put on makeup, mascara burning into my eyes, smudging my cheeks so that I looked as if I had been shoveling coal in a basement. I was scrubbing if off when the doorbell rang.

"The door, Mom!"

"Get it, Matthew!"

"What?"

"Get it!"

Drying my face on a towel, I heard Conrad come in.

"Where's your mother, Matthew?"

"Oh, she's here."

I felt sick with a watery sickness, my life flowing away from me. Gone almost gone. I stepped out of the bathroom into the hall that ran from the living room into the rest of the apartment. It was a narrow place, a close, constricted little passageway. Conrad stood facing me in the entrance to the living room. He seemed jammed into that space, filling it up almost completely. It was as if he had become huge, all his S familiar proportions suddenly swollen.

"Why did you do it, Molly?"

"Because I've had enough, Conrad! I've had enough—do you understand?"

In fact, I hadn't had enough. No, not even by then. Neither enough to sustain me, nor to force me to the point where I could contemplate giving Conrad up—both my need to be loved and my capacity to hang on without proof of it being larger than I ever would have suspected at the time.

So if I remember screaming various things at him in that hallway—all the bitter accusations one is supposed to give vent to in such circumstances—I also must acknowledge the lack of conviction behind those utterances, the sense of all my words somehow falling short of the mark. It was only a false showdown in the end. I could not bring myself to make the ultimate threat—the removal of my person, my physical and psychic self, from his life.

Oh, he had me there, Conrad did—and he knew it. Nor did he hestitate to seize the advantage this gave him. Now was when he chose to inform me, for example, that my brief defection to Fred had hurt him severely—quite apart from its consequences. Since I'd been married to the man in question, he'd felt it wasn't his proper role to call me to account for what I'd done. But the incident had made him wonder whether he could ever rely on me absolutely. Perhaps our sensibilities weren't as well matched as he'd once thought.

"You're much too volatile, Molly. I can see how you can even be vengeful. In this instance you acted without consulting me and hurt a person whose feelings I consider terribly mportant."

"Fuck you, Conrad! I wasn't about to consult you!"

"You see, Molly—you see how given to extremes you are! I know you're not in a state to believe this, but I was about to talk to Roberta myself. I thought she was almost ready to hear what I had to say about the situation and even come to where she could accept it."

"What situation did you mean her to accept? You said months ago, *months ago*, Conrad, that you and I would be together."

"I never made any specific promises. We all have our own timetables."

"You did make promises. You did!"

"Hairsplitting. What we should consider is our mutual lack of trust—and whether that gives us any basis to continue."

Intellectually, of course, the answer should have been no. With a sob I ran to him. It mattered much less now why he had gone to Philadelphia. Only the fact that even so, he hadn't meant to let go of me was significant. If the danger of losing him had not existed before, my own act—even if morally justified—had brought it into being. I had made a perhaps fatal error in strategy.

He proposed a moratorium. A moratorium of two months without contact. Some time in February we would reassess the situation. It was a period of concern about the bombings in Cambodia and the term *moratorium* was very much in the air.

I remember running after him as he walked toward the door, shouting that this was nothing either of us wanted, that it was a juvenile and artificial solution.

"It may be artifical and juvenile, Molly, but I absolutely insist on it."

The front door opened and closed behind him. The elevator was waiting and took him down.

There is no relief for a painful relationship as immediately effective as another painful relationship. I say this with as much conviction as irony, thinking of Malcolm whom I have not yet mentioned, whom I still remember with anguish. There are still certain streets on Broadway in the Eighties that I try to avoid whenever possible now that I have moved further uptown, so imbued are they with memories of our accidental meetings that always seemed more than chance occurrences—he walking his dog, Shadow, I lugging my cart of groceries. Nor will I pass, if I can help it, a certain hillside in Riverside Park that we frequented one spring, planted with cherry trees sent over from Japan as a postwar gesture of goodwill. It is odd that it is Malcolm, whose relationship with me was much more fleeting and insubstantial than the one with Conrad, about whom I have this disturbing sense of lingering presence. Sometimes I have the feeling that we will inevitably meet again. He will appear before

113

my eyes at some point in the future, a gaunt, apocalyptic figure in an embroidered shirt picked up during his travels with his nineteen-year-old girlfriend in Nepal. I will note the further incursion of gray in his overlong hair, the beads around his neck—and that, finally, will be the end.

I fell in love during Conrad's moratorium. It was not that loving Malcolm I fell out of love with Conrad, but that I now found myself with two love objects, both mercurial and tantalizing, each differently unsatisfying. Together the two might have made up one entire person, the perfect lover of my fantasies. I would have settled for either.

Does this indicate a person of shallow emotions? A fickle, inconstant creature—such as women left to their own devices were once traditionally viewed to be? I have already shown myself to be jealous and vindictive. What other base qualities shall I acknowledge? A vulnerability to certain types of men?

No doubt in the old people's nursing home, I will meet a failed poet, still handsome in his declining years, brilliant and bitter-mouthed—a withered lecher to whose room I will carry bowls of unappreciated fruit in my softly wrinkled hands, seeded rolls stolen from the table and wrapped in napkins. I will find things to admire in each of his poems. The imagery of one, the rhythm of another. Never the two together—but I will not mention that. Just as I will try to overlook his pathetic flirtation with the recreation director, for whose eyes he will write verse of appalling triviality. I will still know that I am the sensitive one, the one who truly understands, the secret sharer.

I met Malcolm at a demonstration in Foley Square in support of the Mahwah Seven, whose trial was shortly to begin. Honesty compels me to admit that I attended that

demonstration for motives that were not entirely political. Conrad, who was the lawyer for one of the defen-
dants, had been listed in the *Village Voice* as one of the
speakers. I had not heard from him for several weeks.

As I traveled downtown on the subway during my
lunch hour, I ran through various scenarios. I would
show up for his speech and take pains to bury myself in
the crowd. Looking up at him on the courthouse steps, I
would notice an unmistakable pallor, perhaps even
weight loss. As his eyes swept over his rapt listeners, he
would accidentally notice me. For just a moment words
would fail him; he would resume with a hoarseness in
his voice and a lack of continuity in his argument. I
would slip away to the IRT.

Another version involved Roberta. In this one I walked
boldly and deliberately over to where the two of them
were standing. "Don't you have the guts to say hello,
Conrad?"

I felt slightly nauseous as I got off the subway. Wasn't I
invading Conrad's territory without his sanction? And
yet this was a public event, I told myself angrily. Anyone
had the right to participate. Indeed posters had gone up
all over the city soliciting support. COME JOIN YOUR
BROTHERS AND SISTERS AT THE COURTHOUSE. THIS IS
YOUR STRUGGLE.

There was only a small group of demonstrators, maybe
thirty or forty people—not the large crowd I had imagined. As I walked through the line of police, I tried to
fight off the feeling of illegitimacy that assailed me. I was
aware how much I looked like what I was in part—a person with a respectable job uptown who had just left her
desk for an hour, wearing a stylish red plaid coat that was
only seeing its second season, her hair lightly but guiltily
sprayed with an ozone-depleting conditioner, her com-

plexion painted with byproducts of the petroleum industry. I felt lonely among the army surplus jackets, the pale, fervent, unembellished faces. Clearly the revolution when it came was to be done in shades of brown. Those who refused to give up the primaries, the soft pastels, would be objects of suspicion. Even Conrad felt uneasy about my use of eye shadow, although he admired the effect. I wondered if Roberta wore olive drab, foreswore lipstick, just to please him. I looked for her among the army jackets. I looked for a large redheaded figure on the steps above me, where the speakers were.

It was drizzling. Magic Marker bled down the signs people were holding aloft. There was an attempt to get everyone to burst into song—"We Shall Overcome." I opened my mouth but no sound came forth—I felt paralyzed by the kind of shyness that used to come over me in school assemblies. A tall man who had been looking me over for a while laughed. "I've always hated public singing," I said somewhat angrily.

"So have I. What do you suppose there is about it?"

"Fear of singing flat."

He was quite a pleasing looking man. Narrow gray eyes behind rimless glasses, sandy hair tied back neatly—he looked a bit like a Founding Father of our country. "No, there's more to it than that," he said. "Fear of joining. A desire not to become merged."

"But actually I would like to be."

"One can want both," he said reasonably.

When I knew Malcolm better, I realized how characteristic it was of him to strike up a conversation with a stranger—always seeking the intense chance encounter that would perhaps reveal to him the mystery of himself. A man who lived in his head or in the streets, never comfortably in anybody's living room, including his own.

116

Perhaps it was my unmergedness that attracted him, the red of the coat I wore that day.

Conrad never showed up. I learned later that he had been planning to fly in for the demonstration from Buffalo where he'd been doing some fund raising, but had overslept and missed his plane by fifteen minutes. As in many acts of fate, there was in my meeting with Malcolm an element of the predictable.

I didn't go back to work that afternoon. I called in sick from a phone booth outside the coffee shop where Malcolm and I had taken shelter from the downpour that ended the demonstration. We had by that time exchanged histories as well as other things that were unspoken—certain looks and gestures open to interpretation, indicating more than met the eye. We talked about displacement—we were both lately come from failed marriages, people starting over again. It was his candor that drew me—his life spread open among the coffee cups. I didn't tell him about Conrad.

He had left his wife two years ago. He had a son who was having a painful late adolescence in which he felt powerless to intervene. His wife was the daughter of a university president—he had married her after knowing her a week, enacted the respectability she demanded. He had been a tenured professor of literature at Vassar. Now he was teaching creative writing to black prisoners at Greenhaven, living in a basement apartment rent-free in return for janitorial services. The very austerity of his existence was a source of exhilaration for him, freeing him from a guilt he'd carried secretly all his adult life, ever since he, the son of dirt-poor working-class parents, had gone to Princeton on a full scholarship.

"Only in the recognition that we are all prisoners of so-

117

ciety is there the possibility of freedom." Across the Formica table, Malcolm's gray eyes, slightly enlarged by
thick glass lenses, fixed on mine.

Compelling words—even though I knew that particular recognition was not unique to Malcolm. It was carried
in the air of the time, so to speak, usually mouthed as a
sign of solidarity with what Conrad liked to call the
Lumpen Proletariat. It was something else again to take
it unto oneself as Malcolm had. Conrad would never
have embraced such despair.

At the thought of Conrad, I felt a pang, a sharp ache in
the flesh. Or was it the presence of Malcolm? Matching
him candor for candor, I said that as a woman I was not
only a prisoner of society but of biology as well—that I
admitted my ability to make choices was limited by the
latter. My head was swimming slightly.

It was shortly afterward that we stood up from the table to go our separate ways—the die was not yet cast. He
touched the sleeve of my coat, ran his fingers up and
down the closely piled fabric. "You look so warm in
that," he said.

I stood stock still, wondering whether I was experiencing a caress. I said something lame and idiotic. "Well, it
keeps the cold out."

His hand, no longer in motion, rested on my sleeve
with what now seemed deliberate intention. "What I
would like," he murmured, "is for us to spend the rest of
this day together."

The clock above the cash register said it was only two-
thirty. In three hours the baby sitter would be bringing
Matthew home. I wondered in the back of mind whether
Malcolm and I would have made love by then.

It was still raining outside and so we didn't go for a
long walk as we might have done—as we often did, in
fact, later in our relationship. Instead I invited him to

accompany me uptown, which turned out to be quite convenient for him since his house was only four blocks from mine.

I knew what I was doing, why I was inviting him. I wanted to break the seal Conrad had set upon my emotions, my sexuality. As each day passed, I had become more and more incensed by the so-called moratorium. It seemed the very betrayal of passion. For is it not the nature of passion to flow like an unregulated stream, rather than to be confined and measured, to be tested in deliberate cooling-off experiments? It was the grand flow that I wanted from Conrad and never got.

I wonder now if there might have been something generalized in that desire, if it was free-floating, so to speak—ready to attach itself with a rather astonishing ease to whatever object drifted into its path.

For obvious reasons, I prefer not to call it desperation.

Despite everything that happened afterward—or didn't happen—I still see that first time with Malcolm as a joyful adventure. "I would like us to go into your bedroom," he said after we had sat drinking coffee on the living-room couch long enough. I appreciated his way of stating things very simply—"I would like" or "I would not like." The gap between what he was saying and what he was thinking seemed narrower than with most people. If he'd asked me whether *I* wanted to make love with him, I would, out of perverse female convention, probably have said no.

Thus freed from myself, I lay down with him. Our unfamiliar bodies mingled. He was light and hard in my arms. I felt his long bones grind against mine. He entered me fiercely and held me afterward, his head with its graying hair that was much softer than Conrad's, between my breasts.

119

It is decisive for Molly that he calls her the next day—in fact, the morning after. The phone rings just as she is leaving to go to the office.

"How are you?" says a man's voice.

"Oh, I'm fine," she answers, embarrassed because she is not sure at first of the identity of the speaker.

"I'm fine, too. Really fine," Malcolm says warmly. It *is* Malcolm, she is quite positive now. After all, he has never phoned her before.

"I wanted you to know," he says, "that I'm very glad it happened. That's why I'm calling."

She is rendered almost speechless.

"I'm glad, too," she says after a moment. She is amazed by his kindness. Whatever she had expected of him, it had been much less than this.

"Molly, I'd like to see you again very soon. Why don't we have lunch on Thursday?"

Lunch? It is only when she is riding downtown on the subway that she questions the limitations of that arrangement as opposed to dinner.

By Thursday she has alternated a thousand times between expectation and caution. Felicia warns her against optimism. What does she really know about this man? "For all you know," Felicia sensibly points out, "he might be seriously involved with someone."

"Oh yes," she agrees cheerfully. "For all I know."

"You've been wrong before, ducky."

"That doesn't mean I have to be consistent."

Stubbornly Felicia refuses to be impressed by the phone call. "It could merely have been good manners on his part—not that that isn't an unusual quality these days."

There is no way Molly can convey to her friend the exact quality of tone, the tenderness and honesty, with which the words "I want you to know that I'm very glad it happened" were uttered—something quite different than civility that had momentarily transfixed her, as if she were a prisoner finding the door to her cell unaccountably left open.

They have agreed to meet in the lobby at half-past twelve, but she leaves her office ten minutes earlier than she has to. She has the desire to stand down there alone and get her bearings. She will watch people go in and out through the revolving glass doors; finally one of them will be Malcolm.

The elevator opens into the lobby and he is there already, coming forward, saying her name.

"But you're early." She laughs shyly.

"So are you."

"I had to do an errand," she says, embarrassed by the excitement she feels. What if it is visible ?

"Do you want to do it now?"

"It can wait."

He is looking at her with an odd reserve, as if he is gathering himself for some important statement. Then he steps up close to her and kisses her. It is neither passionate nor ceremonious but a small act of defiance—a kiss in the lobby of an office building.

As they leave the building and walk down the street, his arm encircles her shoulders, his fingertips dangling just above her left breast. They are lovers for all the world to see. Her thick winter coat makes the effect less dramatic than it would have been in a warmer season. Bobbing up and down a little against his arm, she tries to adjust her stride to his longer one. She sees herself smiling up at him. They are discussing which restaurant to go to. "Come," he says as they reach the corner, just as the traffic light is about to change to red. The arm that is around her unwraps itself. His hand grips hers, pulling her after him. They race across the street like children, pausing on the other side while she catches her breath. The arm encircles her again.

He is even handsomer than she remembers—or at any rate, she is seeing him with a different intensity. She tells him that she likes *his* coat, which is a suede sheepskin-lined one, no doubt from his professorial days. It is very much stained and softened. Just under his left sleeve, the suede has begun to split downward. She thinks that you could put your fingers in there and feel the warmth of the sheepskin underneath. She imagines them in a room, the one he lives in—a narrow, white low-ceilinged room with very little in it; a low, hard bed in a corner covered by a

123

black blanket tucked under the mattress in a taut, military sort of way. She would like him to kiss her—not here in the street but in that room.

I remember ordering an omelette for lunch, even though I'd had scrambled eggs for breakfast. It was the least expensive item on the menu in the French restaurant where Malcolm had insisted on taking me. For himself he ordered pâté and brochette of veal, an endive salad. "I've managed to hang on to my American Express card," he informed me. "A useful relic." He signaled to the waiter to bring us white wine.

"A carafe, M'sieu?"

"No, make it a whole bottle. You're not eating very much," he said to me.

"I'm trying to give up eating."

I felt protective of Malcolm's austerity, touched by his desire to show me that he could be expansive. He did not have to woo me that way. His spareness seemed the welcome antithesis of Conrad's abundance that overflowed all too often into sloppiness and chaos. Conrad's clothes never grew old and soft like Malcolm's; he'd buy them new and wear them out completely in a few weeks.

Since I could not dislodge Conrad from my consciousness, I included him as a witness now. He was the invisible third party at the table, like the prophet who visits the Passover Feast. He watched me enjoy myself with this delightful man, my new lover, watched me drink the pale wine Malcolm had bought for me, watched us lean toward each other, our foreheads almost touching, as Malcolm fed me a morsel of veal from his plate, popping it into my mouth with the casualness of intimacy—a gesture which belied the careful avoidance of the personal in his conversation.

For though I awaited words from Malcolm in the same vein as those I had heard on the phone, today it was his work in the prison that seemed to preoccupy him totally. Occasionally, in his descriptions of life in Greenhaven, his voice would drop into the low and passionate tone that had had such an instantaneous effect upon me previously. He spoke of the eagerness of his students, the confidences they entrusted to him now that he had been tested, how he had to struggle constantly to communicate that he was no different from any of them, that his rage against society was almost equal to theirs. He had only been more privileged, that was all.

"You sound almost as though you're envious," I said.

"Yes, " he said. "I'm envious. I've never lived an honest life."

"Not even now?"

"I come to them as the teacher. The white teacher. Paid by the state. That's bullshit, isn't it?"

I pointed out that it wasn't entirely bullshit. After all, wasn't he giving them something?

"I'm helping them pass time. I read Rilke with them, Blake, Dostoievsky. Imagine interpreting Dostoievsky to *them.* I'm an embarrassment to myself—a middle-class white dude. Yesterday I spent five hours within those walls. Today I'm sipping wine in a fancy restaurant. With a woman yet!"

"What's wrong with being with a woman?" I said gaily, although it disturbed me to be referred to so abstractly.

He seemed to have to think before he answered. "It's just that I know where *they* are at this moment."

"Is that what you really meant?"

"You think I'm not glad to be with you?" There was that word again. *Glad.* "Fortunate, in fact?" I shook my

125

head, trying to laugh. "Shouldn't I be considered fortunate?" he persisted.

"Only if that's what you consider yourself."

He was looking at me very intently. I reached for more wine.

"I'm wondering whether you'd like to read something," he said.

"Sure. What is it?"

"Something by one of my students—Arnold. Arnold Lewis. I don't know, you might find it offensive."

"I'm not so easily offended."

He took some folded pages out of his pocket, smoothed them out on the table in front of him before he handed them to me.

It was meant to be a poem, I think, although the writer hadn't broken it down into lines. At first, I thought it was a love poem—the writer in his cell imagining "a tall woman walking out in the world," desiring to be loved and held by her. But then he killed her in his mind, systematically mutilating the parts of her that had stirred his fantasies. I read it through with some difficulty to the end.

"Who is Arnold Lewis?" I said. There was a tight, dry feeling in my throat.

"Arnold Lewis is serving twenty years for armed robbery. He's twenty-seven years old." He took the sheets of paper out of my hands. "You look upset," he said.

"It's rather overwhelming. Actually, I hated it."

"But you felt the power in it."

"I'm not sure that it isn't pornography."

"You can't judge someone like Arnold," he said.

"I'm not judging him. When I begin to recover, perhaps I'll feel sorry for him"

126

"It's only fantasy."

"Yes."

"Arnold is one of the sanest people I know. If you met him, you'd probably be charmed by him."

"Undoubtedly," I said bitterly.

"It's a mistake women make, deciding to be sorry for certain men. Perhaps it's a way of cutting them down to size."

I laughed uncomfortably.

"Caught you at it," he said, smiling.

"Should I promise never to feel sorry for you?"

He stared down at the pages he had taken back. "There is something," he said, "I feel I should explain. I showed you Arnold's poem for a reason—aside from the fact that he's important to me. I think we're very similar. I feel that about him more than any of the others. He and I are each locked up in different ways. Arnold manages to express his rage. I respect his rage. It's all he has. He stays alive on it. Mine is something more destructive, something that keeps turning inward if I let it . . . "

"I think you tend to be too self-critical," I suggested.

Malcolm shook his head. "There you are being compassionate. I *like* you, Molly," he said painfully. "It was very good with you."

"I felt the same," I said.

"What I have to tell you is that I don't think it can happen again. I hope you'll be able to accept that. I hate the necessity of having this conversation."

I had trouble focusing on what Malcolm had said to me. It took me a while before I could speak. "Why did you call me if you didn't want to see me?"

"You're someone I wanted to know."

127

I asked him the obvious question, of course, the one I should have originally put to Conrad.

"Are you involved with another woman?"

"You don't understand, Molly. I can only make love with women who are absolute strangers. I'm not someone who gets involved."

I didn't see much of Malcolm for a while after that. At least, we never met by prearrangement. Maybe because I looked for him, I'd run into him now and then. I'd be walking somewhere in the neighborhood and suddenly there he'd be turning the corner and coming toward me. He'd smile and wave. We'd always touch when we reached each other, and I'd find myself feeling obliged to account to him for my sudden presence in his path—"I'm just on the way to Food Fair to pick up a few things. We seem to have run out of nearly everything." A couple of times he walked me all the way to the door of my house but wouldn't come up. He always had his dog with him, a nervous loping creature, given to unpredictable displays of macho ferocity.

I saw Malcolm with another woman once. I was waiting to cross Broadway and the two of them were standing on the other side engaged in conversation. She was a tall

young woman wearing shorts in the middle of winter, a
rabbit's fur jacket, platform shoes. The dog was pulling
on the leash and Malcolm kept jerking it back impatiently. I changed my mind about crossing right there and
went on a few extra blocks.

Conrad called me early in February.

"Hi, Molly."

There was all that familiar cheer again, that total assur-
ance. Had he ever doubted that he would simply find me
there when he was ready—unchanged and waiting. He
gave me a full report on his favorite subject, his most recent activities on the left. The progress of the Mahwah
Seven trial, the article prominently mentioning him that
was about to appear in *Newsweek,* an invitation to speak
at Harvard in the spring. On a somewhat more intimate
level, he reported on the declining condition of his car,
the current mental health of his mother.

Nonetheless, there was comfort in this conversation.
The calm of neutrality descended upon me like a drug,
momentarily robbing me of my defenses. I considered
actually confiding in him in the same matter-of-fact
tone—telling him how hurtful his two-month silence had
been to me, how I had at first counted off the days of our
abstinence like a child counting off the days till Christmas, and how I'd felt bereft in a different way ever since
I'd met Malcolm, inhabiting a fantasy existence of trou-
bling intensity wherein Malcolm and I bedded down
again and again just as we had that first and only time, his
movements and mine formalized by now into a slowed-
down elaborate dance. It was the kind of conversation I
could have had with Felicia. But Conrad was not my
friend.

Finally I said, "But how have you *been,* Conrad?"

There was a pause, and then he said in a reluctant
voice, "Well, I've missed you."

I suppose that was what I wanted to hear.

I got over there fast enough that night. He said his back was hurting and he couldn't come out, but he wanted very much to see me.

I left the dinner dishes unwashed in the sink. I phoned a neighbor with whom I had a slight acquaintance. She was a mother of three who'd hardly notice one more child, I thought. I asked her if she'd mind watching Matthew for a couple of hours. How resourceful I was in the service of madness. I told her my fiancé was seriously ill. "Oh dear," she said. "Do you think he will require hospitalization?" I said I hoped it wouldn't come to that.

I remember Matthew tearful in the elevator we took to her apartment. Above all things, small children desire consistency. It takes maturity to develop a taste for the impossible, as well as the willingness to rush after it at the drop of a hat.

"I didn't expect you so soon," Conrad said after he had opened the door.

There was a pleased look on his face that made me wish I had arrived much later.

"Well, I can't stay long."

Smiling, he kissed me, quick to thrust his tongue between my lips. "Come in," he said. "I'm on the phone."

"Naturally."

"There's just one more call that I'm expecting and then I'll take it off the hook."

"I wouldn't dream of asking such a sacrifice."

He left me in the front hallway of the apartment, then limping slightly, headed back toward the kitchen. I stood there taking off my coat, all my attention focused upon an object I had never seen before in Conrad's house—the newest feature, so to speak. It was a female bicycle. An ordinary black bicycle that might have been the twin to the one that Conrad owned himself. Jauntily embellished with a basket, it stood side by side with its male counterpart with an air of complete self-possession, as if they were a pair of long standing. I had an urge to shake it by its handlebars and knock it down.

Slowly I advanced into the living room, scanning it for further signs of invasion. It looked reassuringly much the same. Only the piles of books and papers had changed their configurations. The dust was as thick as ever. Finally I spotted what I was looking for—a small pepper plant on a window sill. A gift no doubt, since Conrad had very little interest in horticulture. I noted that it had lost three quarters of its leaves. Four remaining purple and magenta peppers clung to its withering stem. Clearly it had been neglected for at least a week.

Attached to the telephone cord by the receiver cradled under his chin, Conrad emerged in the small archway that led from the kitchen. He held up a bottle of beer and a glass and made pouring gestures. I nodded affirmatively and again he disappeared from view. Finally I heard the click of the receiver, the slamming of the refrigerator door and various clinking and rummaging sounds, followed by the vision of Conrad himself slowly bearing in a battered tin tray on which there were two glasses of beer and a bag of pretzels. He had a look on his face of rather consciously boyish charm, as if he knew there is nothing more endearing to a woman than a large helpless man struggling with the little chores of domesticity.

"Your plant needs watering," I said, thinking we might as well get down to basics.

"Oh, that's right. I seem to keep forgetting it." He set the tray down on the coffee table in front of me, wincing as he straightened up.

"I think they need watering every two days."

He smiled at me through his pain in innocence and tenderness. "I'll try to remember," he said.

"But that one looks as though it's too far gone."

He sat down next to me on the couch and took my hand. His round and cheerful face descended toward mine, then momentarily veered. Very deliberately he breathed into my ear. "Do you think I should throw it out?"

I was a little shocked by his lack of sentiment.

"I would if I were you."

"You have a strain of ruthlessness, Molly," he sighed.

"Along with my capacity to be vindictive."

"I think I might be able to live with that."

I made note of that choice of words. *Live with.*

"But could you live with the rest of me? Isn't that the question?"

I noted that I was being terrifically direct—and wondered what all this noting signified. Perhaps a change in the way in which I cared for Conrad. A real diminishment.

"That's a more difficult one," I heard him say.

I smiled at his predictability.

Turning away from him, I stared at the plant on the window sill. As if it withered under my gaze, a pepper dropped off and fell into the pot with a small dry sound. I found myself laughing. "You've lost another pepper," I said.

He moved closer to me. "Forget the goddamn peppers."

"You know what I wish, Conrad?"

"What do you wish?" he said patiently, as if to a child.

"I wish you were just an old friend I hadn't seen for a while. I wish we could just be—restful."

"The desire to be restful is one that I share. It makes

133

me happy to see you, Molly. I have very warm feelings toward you. I thought we could have a quiet drink, a good talk, see where we're going from here."

"Where *are* we going, Conrad?"

"Well, there've been certain changes."

"There've been certain changes in my life, too," I said quickly. "Certain additions. There's someone I've become preoccupied with." I thought that was the most accurate way of describing my relationship with Malcolm without going into further detail.

"I'm not surprised," he said after a moment. "I'm sure you could have a lot of additions in your life if that was what you wanted. I don't think you even know how attractive you are."

"I have short legs," I said.

"What are you talking about?"

"That's what Fred always used to tell me."

"Well, Fred is a fool."

"Actually, I look like my grandmother. They're the kind of legs that run in the family."

"Molly, certainly you've never doubted that I found you attractive."

I could feel happiness about to sneak up on me any minute. I tried to steel myself against it. "No," I said. "There've been different problems."

Closing his eyes wearily, Conrad sank back against the pillows at the other end of the couch. "My back happens to be killing me," he said.

"I'm sorry." Reaching out slowly, I put my hand on his forehead, covered his closed eyes.

"That's friendlier," he murmured.

"Did you do something to it? Or is it tension?"

"Tension," he said.

134

"Are these changes you mentioned before making you tense?"

"Yes," he said grimly.

"I told my neighbor you were seriously ill. That was how I got out." I moved my hand down his face, gently rubbed the side of his neck. "Does that make you feel any less tense?"

"To tell you the truth, my back hurts like hell at the moment. But it's nice you're doing what you're doing."

"Oh, I can be nice."

"I know you can, Molly."

"May I ask you just another small question?"

"If it's a nice question."

"Is the bicycle a permanent fixture?"

"The bicycle?"

"The one that isn't yours, the one in the hallway. I'm really trying to forget the peppers, but I keep remembering the bicycle."

"Roberta thought it would make sense to leave it here for a while. She goes riding a lot in Central Park even at this time of the year."

"I see. Maybe I'll get one myself and leave it here too if there's room. Except mine will probably be yellow."

"Molly, you've told me you don't even know how to ride."

"Well, you could teach me. Is the bicycle going to be followed by anything else I should know about?"

"What do you mean?"

"I mean other possessions of Roberta's. Roberta herself."

He sighed—more heavily this time. "I was getting to that," he said. "What's actually happening is that Roberta's bicycle is going to go away. It won't be here the next time you come. She's picking it up tomorrow. She's very angry with me."

"Angry? After having you all to herself for two months?"

"I'm not the easiest person to get along with. I have many faults that can be annoying on a day-to-day basis. Still Roberta has become convinced that we should live together. She thinks that's the only way to resolve many of our problems."

For a moment I could scarcely breathe. "And you don't feel the same," I said.

"I'm not at a point where I'm ready to make that commitment to anybody."

"But if you did, it would be to her."

"I didn't say that, Molly."

"No, I said it."

"Molly, don't you think my feelings for you have quite a lot to do with all of this?"

"I don't really know anything, Conrad."

"Then you should allow your own instincts to tell you something."

"Lately I've been trying not to have any instincts. I'd just like to exist in a realm of fact for a change." Actually, it was Malcolm I was thinking of as well as the situation at hand. I wondered if I'd even be making such statements to Conrad now if it hadn't been for what had happened with Malcolm, too.

Conrad was looking at me meanwhile in a soft sort of way, as if he sincerely wanted to show me he understood. "What would you say, Molly, if I told you Roberta and I have decided to stop seeing each other—and that there is a seventy-five percent chance that this is a permanent decision?"

"I'd say," I said, still curiously unable to breathe nor-

136

mally, "that I'd still have to worry about the other twenty-five percent."

"Twenty-five percent is just a generous allowance for outside possibilities. I know your desire for me to be honest. But wouldn't you say the odds are in your favor—assuming of course that you still want to have me? I know nothing about your relationship with this other person."

"I still want to have you, Conrad," I said after a while.

He drew me down to him and kissed me, holding me against him. "I hope you're prepared to see a lot of me. I'm going to be very lonely, you know."

There are times when words run away from us. Even the most persuasive orator, the brilliant negotiator, the expert weaver and dodger, can make a slip. A faltering of attention, a moment of ambivalence, and we are apt to say the totally inappropriate thing—or to be more honest than we ever intended. Conrad was not exempt from this weakness. That incongruous remark about being very lonely was one of the most revealing things he ever allowed himself to say to me.

At first I noted it as incongruous—nothing more. My mind was adjusting to the realization that I had won, and I wondered why the victory seemed so undramatic. Why there was a dullness of feeling, when one might have expected exhilaration. I suppose I had always imagined that at some point Conrad would consciously choose me. Instead I felt rather like a consolation prize, what was left to Conrad in the wake of Roberta's defection. Since I was already there, he had me to fall back on. But why even then would he say he'd be lonely? It was an effect of stress like his backache. Perhaps I was wrong to expect too much from him. Whatever his less positive feelings had been for Roberta, he had undoubtedly become very used to her. With her terrible dependency she had filled his life, confirmed his sense of his own importance. Maybe Conrad didn't feel important at all, and thus needed confirmation over and over again from as many different sources as possible. He was vulnerable, my Conrad. Perhaps you had to keep going down to get to that place in him—but it was there.

I felt a tenderness for him. The brittle game of words I'd been playing suddenly ended. Lying in his arms, I whispered to him that he was not to worry about being lonely.

If there is one thing I have always believed in, it is the inability of men to know their own minds. Putting my faith in this negative side of their character, I have acted accordingly—not always with success. I believed, for example, that I could turn Fred into a father by the very act of producing a baby. It was I who promised nothing would change—and he who kept his side of the bargain to the letter. Still I have my son, the one male in my life with whom I have a permanent relationship. Other miscalculations have left me with less.

Is it better not to win at all than to win by default? Whatever the answer to that question, it was not in me to have walked away from Conrad at that juncture. Perhaps Isabel Archer could have done it. There was a time when I was much younger when the novels of Henry James had considerable influence upon my notion of morality. It was that repeated Jamesian act of renunciation that became for me almost a religious ideal. The summer I was nineteen I seriously wanted to be Lambert Strether. Instead I grew up and became the person I am.

I have found it nearly impossible most of the time to live my life by absolute standards. It is more a matter of getting by, making do with what one has—improvising recklessly out of some misguided belief in one's ability to prevail. I present myself to the world with a rather self-effacing exterior. Perhaps underneath there is a blind and stubborn arrogance.

It was like a marriage, she thought after a while, in the sense that Conrad could be absent in the very midst of being present in the way that husbands often are. At least that had been her own experience of marriage, although she retained hopes that it need not necessarily be universal. At any rate, they did not seem very much like lovers. This was partially due to the fact that even after Conrad had recovered from his back ache, they made love on an average of only once a week, usually for some reason Thursdays—though they now spent four or five nights together, including weekends.

He talks about being tired so much, she begins to worry he may indeed be in danger of burning himself out— an expression he uses once when he feels particularly depressed. Another time he tells her, "I feel depleted." She does not really think that it is her fault, but she tries to be very understanding. Soft-spoken with him now, never caustic or demanding. She is troubled by something apologetic in this behavior, but once she has assumed it, it seems to overwhelm her normal personality. Often when she is with him, she feels muted, dim—missing the sense of herself that used to come in the midst of combat or in the devious subtleties of interrogation. Yet it was she who'd wanted things to be restful.

Actually, she believes that this restfulness, if she can

141

only sustain it, will eventually restore him. Roberta in this situation might have become hysterical. Molly, on the other hand, is the exemplar of quiet patience.

Much of her time and energy is spent in the preparation of food. She consults books on international cuisine and follows out elaborate recipes, requiring the mincing and chopping of many different ingredients. Getting started on dinner early in the evening, she puts things on the stove or in the oven, adjusting the cooking temperature down or up or removing the dish in question from the heat altogether, depending upon the arrival time specified in the phone call from Conrad that invariably comes at the very moment she had expected him to sit down at her table. She becomes an expert at keeping things warm for him without drying them out, although it often hardly matters. He is apt to eat ravenously but with a kind of obliviousness—chewing abstractedly as he makes his innumerable late night phone calls, following up the loose ends of meetings, apologizing for appointments missed during the day, making mysterious arrangements to go to other cities, to be picked up at airports, to be put up in houses—because he never stays at a hotel if he can help it, and there seems to be no end to the number of people who desire to put him up, whether upstate, in the Midwest or in the New England area. All these people are in the Movement, and they are all described to her as "one of my good friends." "I never meet your friends," she remarks from time to time, and he says, yes, isn't it a shame she's so tied down, he'd take her with him otherwise. But then, most of his trips are so short, they'd hardly be worth the money they'd cost her or the trouble of making arrangements.

They watch the Late Show and go to bed. His eyes start to close almost as soon as he lowers his head to the pillow. He rolls away from her to the far side of the mattress. She contemplates his massive back, the various freckles and moles upon it, the ridge of red hair that runs down the center, and then, finally, turns off the light.

"Have you noticed," I said one day, "that you and I hardly ever make love any more?"

"Oh, I don't think you could call it hardly ever," he said. "But I have noticed. When was the last time?"

"Two weeks ago," I said.

"It wasn't as long ago as that."

"Well, it was."

"Do you keep a chart?" he said bitterly.

Tears instantly streamed out of my eyes.

"Molly," he said tiredly, "I'm going through some kind of transitional period."

"Are you really sure it's just transitional?"

"For some reason I feel a lack of desire. I don't feel sexual with you right now. If it disturbs you, maybe we should see each other less."

I said it didn't disturb me violently. It just disturbed me a little.

One night I dreamed about Conrad and Roberta. I dreamed I was walking down the blank and unending corridors of a hotel—sort of a Hilton of the imagination. All the identical doors were closed except one. This one opened upon a room from which music issued. Looking in, I saw that a wedding was in progress. It was the wedding of Conrad and Roberta—a Jewish wedding complete with canopy, chopped liver, and the traditional glass that was to be broken by the groom, which stood elevated and separate on a special little table. The guests, drinking wine and enjoying themselves, were all in olive drab and denim. "Come in," they urged me. And even Conrad turned for a moment and said, "Why don't you come in, Molly?" But I stood in the doorway and would go no farther.

When I related this dream to Conrad, he said it just proved how deeply our early conditioning was rooted in our subconscious, so that even our dreams took on stereotypical capitalist forms. As to my anxiety relating to his going back to Roberta, he reminded me of his honesty in establishing his original ratio of sixty:forty.

"Seventy-five!" I cried out in correction.

"A figure of speech, Molly. What are we really talking about anyway? People you've been very close to don't simply drop out of your consciousness—" he paused and gave me a long, deliberate look—"or even out of your life," he said.

"Oh, have you been seeing her?" I tried to get the words out very evenly.

"We keep in touch. She's decided now that what she really wants to do is go to law school. Naturally, she came to me for advice."

"Who else?"

"She's calmed down considerably about her relationship to me. A lot was set in motion when you called her, Molly. I was very upset at the time, but actually it forced a great many clarifications to the surface. I see it now as probably constructive for her, although I know that was not your intention."

"I just wanted everyone to know the truth, Conrad."

"But you took out your anger on her. I still find that disturbing. Maybe that's why there's blockage now in some of my feelings."

"Will it go away?" I asked very quietly.

"I certainly hope so. I don't intend to remain in this state indefinitely."

* * *

We talked very openly now about Conrad's state. Once we had named it, it became a subject between us. We no longer called it exhaustion but blockage. It was as if the name gave the condition a certain density. I felt it as something palpable—a perceptibly increasing mass. It took its place among the dishes on the table, located itself in the very center of the bed. I was constantly aware of its presence in the excruciating way I was aware of Conrad himself—his hand brushing against mine when he reached for the salt, the very slight amount of pressure in the quick kiss he gave me late one night when I greeted him at the door and he was tired and forgetful for a moment. I would watch him as he wrote on his long yellow pads or read the newspaper, registering the turning of a page in the pores of my skin, waiting for him to look up across the room.

Gloom settled upon him, bringing with it a certain sweetness I had not seen in him before. He became peculiarly considerate—complimenting me on even the simplest meals, insisting on washing the dishes. Once he amazed me by mopping the bathroom floor, knocking over an entire bucket of water in the process. Almost ritualistically he would ask me about my day at the office. "You know your mother works very hard," he would remind Matthew, lecturing him from time to time on cooperation and responsibility. It pleased Conrad to view me as a worker—and therefore oppressed.

Perhaps he was afraid I might desert him. He began coming over every night of the week, sometimes turning up without warning or calling me in the small hours of the morning and telling me he was on his way. Now he would want me to hold him before he fell asleep. "Would you like me to make you hard?" I'd whisper. Most of the time I couldn't.

There was one week he didn't go back to his apartment at all. He bought a package of underwear and rinsed the same shirt out every other night. He gave my number to his answering service. Finally on Sunday afternoon he said he thought he'd go and pick up his mail. "Would you mind walking over there with me?" he said. We took Matthew with us. It was a warm day at the very end of winter. Conrad was determinedly gay as we walked, turning his attention toward Matthew. He was teaching him a song—"Solidarity Forever." "So-li-DAH-rity," Matthew pronounced it for some reason.

I hadn't been at the apartment for quite a while. It had a desolate look, as if no one really lived there—it was a storage place of castoff clothes, books, unopened correspondence. "We won't stay long," Conrad said. "I just want to throw out the stuff that's in the refrigerator." He was in the kitchen when the doorbell rang—one short tentative ring at first and then a long, insistent one.

"Shall I get it?" I called.

"No, I will." Drying his hands on a dishtowel, Conrad walked to the door. He opened it and stood in the entrance, blocking my view of his visitor. "You shouldn't have come without calling," I heard him say. "There's someone here with me."

I knew instantly who it was that was standing outside. I felt the cruelty of that greeting he gave her. But what else could he have done? It would have been worse, I supposed, to have let her in. I wondered why he couldn't bring himself to say my name to her. What was there left to conceal at this point?

I really wanted to see her. I still had no precise face for her in my mind. Her features were always blurry in my memory of our one encounter.

He was standing so that all that was visible from where

146

I sat was a long shank of black hair, the sleeve of a dark brown quilted jacket.

He stepped out into the hall, closing the door behind him softly but very fast. I could hear the rise and fall of their voices, hers much fainter than his most of the time, now and then inaudible, once just for a moment a high and piercing tone. I couldn't make out the words.

He rang the doorbell after she was safely gone, and I let him in. He stood there distractedly tugging at his hair, trying to look composed. "That was Roberta," he said. "She happened to be in the neighborhood, so she biked over. There was something she needed to ask me."

It's odd to think that's all I ever saw of her.

There was a night that spring that I couldn't stay in the house. Conrad wasn't due until late and Fred had taken Matthew. It unsettled me to be alone. I had no plans. I decided to go for a walk finally—I wasn't sure where. Broadway seemed logical. I went several blocks looking in shop windows, thinking perhaps I'd buy something. It was hard to know what I wanted. I remembered a blue shirt I'd seen in the window of a store that always stayed open late—and was indeed open when I passed it without even stopping, without even choosing not to stop, walking briskly as if with determination, my hands clenched in the pockets of my jacket, my mouth choked with heaviness. To be aimless in the city is to risk being a victim.

It was an evening that invited languor—a softness in the air, the smell of the river blowing up the cross streets—sweet, muddy and rotten. Subterranean, like the smell I always associate with basements. The river itself could be seen, looking west from any corner, gleaming beyond the trees in Riverside Park, the lights of Jersey reflected in its waters.

I left Broadway and headed down in that direction. There was still a little light left in the sky but it was getting swiftly darker. I waited for a break in the traffic and crossed over to the park, passing the winos and derelict old people sitting fearfully on its rim, turning onto a path that led downward toward its empty, unkempt lawns, its silent playgrounds, walking faster as I passed a basketball court where a group of boys stood idly along an iron fence drinking beer as they waited their turn to play. "Hey baby . . . Come here, little pussy . . . *Muchacha* . . ."

I cried when I came upon the cherry trees. There was a whole little hillside of them in full bloom at the point where the park is bisected by the entrance to the highway. A streetlamp shone upon the pink and white flowers massed upon the branches. They shifted on their delicate stems in the gentlest currents of air, scented the river smell with their freshness. I felt the meagerness of my existence, the narrowness of the path I traveled every day of my life, the unendurable waiting, the accumulated burden of unexpressed desires. I had only to veer slightly away from the ordinary to see it. When was I ever so foolish as to walk in the park at night? I was thirty-six and would be thirty-seven. My life extended into the future in its essential sameness, only narrowing perhaps even more.

I stared bitterly at the trees and at the dim lawn at the bottom of the hill where a man was exercising his dog, running with it in circles, stopping now and then to pick up a stick and toss it for the dog to fetch, the circles extending, coming closer. They passed under a light at the base of the hill, and I saw that the man was Malcolm. I called out to him and he climbed the hill and came toward me, stopping under the trees. I thought he looked pleased if anything, not even particularly surprised.

"I decided I'd take a walk," I said, feeling the usual obligation to explain my movements to him. The dog sniffed my legs, making me feel absurd.

"Shadow!" he called warningly.

"It's a good night for it," he said. "Do you come here often?"

"No. Just tonight, in fact. Probably not again."

"Something's wrong?" he asked kindly, coming closer. "You have a look . . ." he said.

I shrugged. "Restlessness," I said. "My life is very complicated at the moment. Confining and complicated."

He stared at me through his glasses, then took my hand. "You never did tell me much about yourself . . ."

"There wasn't much opportunity," I said. "I would have gotten to it after a while."

"But this doesn't necessarily have to be the time."

I said I'd rather it wasn't.

"What we should really do," he said, "is look at these trees. This is possibly their peak, this particular evening. It'll be downhill for them from now on."

I said it was the warm weather we'd been having.

Smiling, he reached up for a branch and shook it. A few petals drifted down. "You have some caught in your hair."

"Your fault," I said. "You have some in yours as well."

"Do I?" he said. "Where?" He took the hand he was holding and guided it up toward his head.

I touched him just above his forehead. "Right here," I said.

JOYCE JOHNSON

"You can leave it there," he said in a low voice.

I think it was I who kissed him then, although we moved toward each other at more or less the same time. Perhaps the hunger in me made me swifter by a moment. Perhaps enough time had elapsed so that I was strange to him again. He told me that passing by the hillside earlier, he'd thought it would be good to be with a woman there. "I'm glad it's you," he said.

We lay down under the trees, he on top of me, pressing me into the damp ground and the dead leaves of winter, an occasional blossom falling upon us like the first trace of an unseasonable snow.

I have a purple nightgown I've worn only once, the most expensive piece of lingerie I've ever owned. It dips low with a keyhole effect in the front and is essentially backless. It's not something anyone would wear for warmth. I bought it for $29.98, thinking it would appeal to Conrad—who'd decided finally the problem was that I didn't know how to be seductive. I just took my clothes off and lay there next to him hoping for the best. More imaginative efforts were necessary at this juncture.

And maybe another problem was that I was boring— not very boring, just a little—my interests being too specifically literary rather than political. Again, the heat of debate might have served to inflame him. My best quality—which always meant a great deal to him, even now—was my supportiveness. That, if only combined with the ability to be stimulating to him both sexually and intellectually, would have made me the perfect companion to share his life.

These conclusions were expressed some time in May during an argument we had after a party he'd taken me to. Leaving me at the cheese table, he'd pretended for the rest of the evening that I was someone he hardly knew—rotating enthusiastically among the other guests, many of whom were Movement friends whom he greeted with fervent embraces, carrying them off to the dance floor where he stomped and shook until the buttons popped off the lower half of his shirt, revealing his navel like a blind cyclopean eye. Nor did he neglect new acquaintances. He had a way of giving a stranger his entire attention, consuming her upturned, fascinated face like the pinkest and most delectable smoked salmon, absorbing her words into the very center of his soul. Occasionally a slip of paper and the stub of a pencil would be drawn from the pocket of his trousers and something would be written down—perhaps a note on some insight of brilliance that had fallen from her lips, perhaps a telephone number. "Schwartzberg's running for office," I heard one woman remark knowingly to another. Occasionally his eyes would meet mine—to be instantly retracted, an innocent glaze coming over them.

Perhaps I read too much into what I saw. I was in an unself-confident period. At any rate, the dark side of my personality came out during the taxi ride home. I accused Conrad of making dates with others. He accused me of morbid suspicion, protesting his virtual monogamy as well as the painful struggle of maintaining it in view of our present difficulties—for which, he had begun to see, I was by no means blameless for the already stated reasons.

It took him a year to make me an apology of sorts, admitting the desperation of that spring, when he'd felt little if anything for any woman. Quite consciously he had tested himself with almost anyone he met, trying to see whether it was possible to locate any feeling of attraction in himself even momentarily.

＊ ＊ ＊

I only half-believed the day I bought the nightgown that once I had it on I would somehow manage to live up to it. I decided to attempt to take Conrad by surprise, appearing in it at a totally unexpected, even seemingly inappropriate time. Surprise was the all-important element in the art of seduction, according to a book I was reading on the subject by a Dr. Hyman D. Ventura. It was a runaway bestseller. I felt shame in even having such a book in the house, let alone having purchased it in a despairing mood for twelve dollars and reading it when I should have been reading Marcuse. Dr. Ventura, whose practice was located in Chula Vista, California, was, I suspected, a frustrated filmmaker—"You are on camera," he would write. "Now for the scenario!" Fading into the bedroom, he would recommend some rather extreme forms of surprise—such as suggesting playfully to one's partner an experiment in bondage. Two and one-half yards of one-inch velvet ribbon were suggested for this purpose, and accompanying diagrams instructed the reader in the tying of various sailor knots that would provide enough pressure to induce excitement without entirely cutting off circulation. One would obviously have to prepare in advance by mastering these complicated knots in secret. So much premeditation seemed dreary. I wondered if the good doctor were aware of the thin line between the seductive and the ludicrous, since it was the maintenance of this fragile boundary that concerned me. The nightgown was about as far as I was prepared to go. I thought I would happen to have it on at dinner rather than reserve it for the hour of retirement. It was a scenario lacking complexity or even much imagination.

I shut myself in my bedroom to try it on a few hours before I expected Conrad. Staring at my reflection skeptically, I cut off the price tags so that I wouldn't be tempted

to return it to the store unworn. My son, coming in un-
ceremoniously to demand his bedtime story, was much
taken with my appearance. "Mom, you look pretty. Sort
of like Cat Woman." He hurled himself upon me in imi-
tation of a wrestling hold he'd seen on television. "Hey
Matthew! Stop acting silly," I protested, laughing un-
easily as I disengaged myself.

I was making beef goulash that night, one of Conrad's
favorite dishes. I put candles on the table, then took them
away. Standing casually in my gown, I stirred the pot
from time to time. I put down the wooden spoon I was
holding when the doorbell rang.

Slowly I walked to the door, the hem of my gown picking up little bits of lint. I kissed him before he even had a
chance to greet me, the nylon fabric crackling with static
electricity. He stepped back from me, averting his eyes
slightly. So much for surprise.

"We have goulash," I said.

In Chula Vista, it might have been chili. In neither case
would Dr. Ventura have allowed such a line to appear in
any of his scripts.

Conrad informed me that he had eaten a hamburger in
the middle of a meeting and wasn't very hungry. Fearing
to expose my backlessness prematurely, I leaned against
the door of the hall closet and said, "Why don't you just
sit down in the kitchen and help yourself to some
wine?"—indicating that I wished him to precede me
there. Once he had sat himself at the table, I walked
swiftly past him to the stove.

"Is this your birthday or some other kind of special occasion?" I heard him say.

"No. What gave you that idea?" Seizing the paprika, I
bent over the pot.

"Well, you seem to have gone to a great deal of trouble."

"Oh, I wouldn't call it trouble." I glanced at him for

just a moment. He was reading the label on the wine bottle with great attention, frowning as he did so. "I just wanted things to be a little different," I said, my voice cracking in an odd way.

I felt relief when there was no response from him. Perhaps he hadn't heard me. I stirred in silence for a while.

"Is that why you have that on?"

I put the dripping wooden spoon down carefully on the counter next to the stove.

"This? This is just something new," I said.

"Different."

"Yes," I said. "Different."

"It's not at all your usual style."

"Maybe my style is changing," I said.

"That's always possible," he said coldly.

I carried the large red pot to the table, brought out the salad of tender greens, the loaf of French bread. As he had warned me, his appetite was poor. There was an air of weariness about him, of melancholy. I almost wished he'd make his usual maddening series of phone calls. He kept his eyes on his plate. Occasionally he'd look up past me with an expression of real pain. Perhaps he read something contemptuous into the act of putting on the gown, as if it were an expression of my impatience rather than an attempt to allure him. And yet I was impatient— nearly desperate by that time—my constant desire for him mixed with bitter anger at his withholding.

He said he had an article to read in a law journal before he went to sleep. He took it with him into the bedroom. I stayed in the kitchen washing the dishes. I wiped off the top of the stove and the front of the refrigerator, I swept the floor and cut back a plant that had become unruly. I felt I wanted to be alone. I went into the living room when I was finished and lay down on the couch, pressing my face against the pillows, drawing my knees up over my belly.

I heard sounds in the middle of the night. Conrad was up, moving around in the rear of the apartment, walking back and forth between the bedroom and the bathroom. Lights were turned on and off. Water ran into the sink. Then I heard his steps in the hall. He walked across the living room and stood beside the couch.

"Are you awake?" he said.

"Yes."

"Well I'm going," he said. "In case you're interested."

"Conrad," I said with difficulty, "I love you." I tried to reach for his hand to hold him back.

"I really want to go home, Molly. I want to be in my own space. I can't see the future."

It is early in the morning and she is at the typewriter because thinking is too circular and painful to be confined inside her head. She has written several letters and thrown them away. It embarrasses her that they all said different things—one expressing a confidence grounded in nothing, another existential despair, one a suspiciously saintly sense of resignation. This will be a last attempt.

Dear Conrad,
    You say you cannot see the future. I feel your pain as keenly as I feel my own. I am sitting here crying because I acted badly and hurt you. Can you understand my feelings of helplessness at all? I should have gone in and held you in my arms, but I was afraid you wouldn't want even that. You are right—I don't know how to be seductive. I only know how to be myself. I am also not always brave.

159

What makes it hard is that I am often overwhelmed with desire for you. It has been that way ever since we met. I have never had such feelings before. Lately I've tried to disguise them so that you wouldn't feel the burden of them so much. Probably that was the wrong thing to do. But then everything I do has seemed wrong lately.

Only my feelings remain clear

She stops, seeing that she has used the word *feelings* three times. The language of love has a limited vocabulary. *What* feelings remain clear? That she has not stopped wanting him and indeed has never wanted him so much as just now when he has been so pitiably humbled, when she feels so terribly sorry for him she has almost forgiven even his cruelty the night of the party— although it is very hard not to take such things personally. Maybe she was unwittingly punishing him with the nightgown after all, flinging his words in his teeth.

She erases the sentence and writes, *I have been so confused*—typing the words in the same space.

I want so much to be close to you, but sometimes I wonder if closeness isn't what you're most afraid of. Oh Conrad, is that the trouble? How could I possibly threaten you?

The words seem to have fallen upon the page. She is stunned, shaken by her own clarity. She thinks of tearing up the letter. But she believes in the power of the truth. Once having found it, one cannot then in conscience back away. She sees herself and Conrad as having become locked as combatants into a war neither of them ever intended. Only with the truth is there the possibility of change.

Please allow me to be close to you now, she writes.

160

That is what we both need—if we are to go on, she adds, then erases that. It is too absolute and therefore ominous as well as false. She realizes that her desire to go on is un-conditional.

The issue of sex is almost inconsequential in comparison, although of course it is part of the same question.

She takes the letter out of the typewriter and signs her name, imagines herself actually sending it—or leaving now and putting it under his door. She sees herself doing that.

She gets dressed very quickly. Going into Matthew's room, she reassures herself that he is still soundly asleep. He will sleep on for nearly an hour. She will be back in twenty-five minutes.

The feeling of clarity fills her, propelling her steps as she walks the eight blocks, the letter in her hand.

She sees him around the corner just as she is putting Matthew on the school bus, hurrying with a lumbering gait that gets faster and more uneven as he approaches— his legs not quite in balance with his heavy body, shirt flapping open, something disorganized about all this effort.

The bus pulls away toward Amsterdam Avenue, Matthew waving from the back window as on ordinary mornings. Faint with hope and apprehension, she tries to raise her hand with a bright mommy-smile—the words of the letter, the words of the letter, printed upon her mind. The strikeouts, the erasures. *But then everything I do has seemed wrong lately.*

"I've read what you have to say, Molly."

She is nodding her head, trembling a little.

161

His voice is hoarse, halting, as if he has not yet caught his breath. "When did you come over?" he asks.

"Early. Very early," she says.

"I was up—but I didn't hear you. I stayed up all last night. Are you going into work now?"

"I'll go in late," she says, looking at him finally, at his gray, creased, unanimated face.

He stares back at her as if through a film, then away as a car passes, followed by a truck.

Stepping forward, she leans against him, shuts her eyes.

He asks her why she hasn't lost all patience. "Isn't it time by now?" he says.

"No."

"But what you said in the letter is probably true. I can't disagree with your analysis. I don't know where that leaves us, Molly."

Tears well up hot behind her eyelids. "Conrad, what are you *feeling*?"

He thinks about it, he considers the question.

"I think I feel like being with you."

It is the tentative phrasing of that sentence that makes her believe him. It is the kind of thing that is so hard for him to say, it is almost out of character—just as writing her the kind of letter she had written him would have been impossible, he admits a little later when they are lying in bed—having definitively completed all that had for a time seemed uncompletable, all blocks having dissolved so quickly it is hard to believe any had ever existed. Hardly anything in his life has ever moved him so much as that letter. He is almost crying as he tells her that.

He says, "My feelings for you are so intense, I can't seem to assimilate them."

She rocks him in her arms. "Then why don't you leave them alone?"

"Isn't that too much to expect?" he says teasingly, his normal good spirits restored.

He assimilates for two days and then—just before the weekend—informs her that he is going back to Roberta.

There is a town upstate called Milton's Crossing, a little to the south of the bridge that crosses the Hudson near Rhinebeck. It is in an area of Dutchess County known for its autumn crop of apples; in the summer a few of the local farmers let out houses—large shingled Victorian structures, the kind that have deep porches with rows of decrepit wicker rockers, upon which one sits in the evenings safe from the mosquitoes beating against the screening. It was such a house that Conrad rented with a group of radical friends and went to live in with Roberta that June, announcing to me his need for space and time in which to "repair damages," as well as his intention of coming into the city as little as possible until September. "I'll keep in touch," he said. He told me he would be staying "somewhere near Saugerties"—a town that happened to be at least thirty miles away and on the other side of the river.

I never told Conrad I once saw the actual house a year after he and Roberta lived there. Any blurring of lines around the compartments in which he kept the various segments of his life disturbed him considerably. It made him nervous enough that we had an acquaintance in common—a young woman named Francine, who'd come to work in my office around the time that Conrad vanished and who'd often been invited by one of her boyfriends to spend the weekend in Milton's Crossing. She had even been asked to join the commune, which she disparagingly called "the orphanage," although she admitted the level of intellectual discussion was high.

Aware of my intense interest in that part of the country, Francine invited me and Matthew for a Sunday drive to the Dutchess County fair. On the way toward the fairgrounds at Rhinebeck, we approached the exit for Milton's Crossing. "Now there's a leading tourist attraction," she said, slowing the car. "Well, would you like to see the place? Or do you think it would upset you?"

I told her I was very curious. Merely curious, I said.

She turned onto a road bordered by fields and orchards—a gently rolling landscape, not mountainous the way it was across the river. The house was painted yellow—which surprised me; I'd imagined it white. There were apple trees on the front lawn with windfallen apples in the uncut grass and hydrangeas were in bloom. The house seemed locked and empty.

Francine pulled into the driveway. "Let's get out," she said, "and I'll show you the view from the back."

I sat for a moment, astonished by the violence of my feelings. I wanted to walk up the steps of the porch, force open the door, walk through every room. *Conrad, I am walking in your house.*

"If anyone comes," I said, "it'll be embarrassing."

"Oh come on. Just for a minute."

166

I followed her out of the car. Matthew ran up the path ahead of us and picked up a long stick to play with. Francine pointed out the withered vestiges of a large vegetable garden which the commune had planted last summer—"Whatever else you want to say about Roberta H., she produces terrific organic tomatoes, and she's a really dedicated weeder"—and a badminton net where there had been games every evening after dinner. "It was an absolute treat to see Conrad in shorts—you know, with that overhanging buddha belly of his—switching away at that little feathered thing. What do they call it?"

"A puck," I said absently, looking out over a meadow that I remembered Conrad had told me he could see from the windows of his bedroom. You could walk across the meadow and into the woods at the edge of it to the swimming hole. It was very private, Francine had said. They all swam naked there.

"No, it's a birdie. A puck is hockey, I believe. Honestly, Molly, it's obvious you're not *sportif.*"

"I didn't know Conrad was."

I was looking at the row of windows on the second floor, wondering which room had been his and Roberta's. I was thinking that I might have been here with him last summer. It might have been me just as well.

"You know what I really admire about Conrad—he doesn't give a damn about being absurd. I mean he's a terrible shit and all—but you sort of have to admire him for that. And for that head of his, I guess."

She was all of twenty-four and her judgments of her elders were delightfully lacking in respect.

I laughed with some uneasiness. "I know what you mean about absurd."

"The trouble with you, Molly, is that you take him seriously."

* * *

167

I was subject to attacks of unreality the summer Conrad went back to Roberta. They would come upon me particularly on my way home from work if I had reason to stop at the supermarket. Why there at the Red Apple, I am not sure. I would push the metal cart down the long aisles, hanging on to it for dear life, in fear that it would glide away from me under its own power before I could choose what I wanted from the shelves—not that I could choose at all, not that I wanted anything. Filled with dread, I would force myself to pick items according to a list I could scarcely remember composing.

It was Conrad's unreachability that filled my mind. I knew that if I could only locate him, I could get him back. Evidently, he knew it as well. Why else would he have taken such pains to hide himself, leaving me not so much as a forwarding address or a phone number, or even listing himself with Information in Saugerties.

I began to go for walks in the evenings—always the same eight blocks down Columbus Avenue. "Let's get a little air," I'd say to Matthew. On the way I'd look at the passing traffic very carefully as well as all the cars that had been parked; perhaps I could spot a green Saab among them. Stationing myself across the street from Conrad's house, I'd look up at his apartment, trying to make out a light behind the drawn blinds and attempting to memorize their current position so that I could tell whether they'd been raised or lowered the next time I came. I'd go upstairs sometimes for an examination of his door. Obviously, he'd asked the doorman to save his mail for him because I never found any outside his apartment. As if I were leaving a note, I'd wedge a folded piece of paper between the edge of the door and the door frame. In a few days, I'd go back and check on it to see if it had been removed. I'd pull it out and crumple it in my pocket. Occasionally, I'd miss an evening and feel convinced that this was the very time he'd come and I'd lost my one chance of confronting him. I'd learned that it was quite useless to leave messages with his office or his answering service.

In July, I rented a two-room cottage in Woodstock, which happened to be near Saugerties. I intended to spend my weekends there, since there was no possibility that Conrad would choose a weekend to come into New York. Since Woodstock happened to be the cultural center of the Catskills as well as the hub of radical activity in that region, it stood to reason that anyone wishing to escape the rural boredom of Saugerties would have to come into Woodstock at least occasionally.

The Woodstock paper printed news of Saugerties from time to time—a square dance at the firehouse sponsored by the American Legion, the discovery of the body of a vagrant who had been shot through the head in a picnic area. I read each item with morbid interest. One event which was widely publicized was Annual Dog Tattooing Day—upon which one could come to the lawn in front of the town hall and have one's dog tattooed with one's Social Security number for a dollar—a free beer for the dog owner thrown in. This epitomized for me the meanness and inanity of that town—and I wondered why Conrad had chosen to spend the summer there, or perhaps it had been Roberta who had made the choice and Conrad with his peculiar obliviousness to what surrounded him had simply gone along with it.

Still I never came upon him in Woodstock, even though I went to all the movies I thought he'd want to see, ate in the restaurants where perhaps he'd take Roberta, attended concerts of his favorite music. I felt as though he deliberately ignored its proximity. Perhaps he'd found out that I was there.

* * *

She has hit upon a way of getting Conrad's phone number in the country—not a very nice way. Still she is quite sure, the moment she thinks of it, that this outrageously awful plan will work. It has to do with making a phone call to Roberta's ex-husband Theodore.

Once she decides to do it, she goes through with it immediately, efficiently looking up the number and writing it down on a little pad, closing the door of her office—the order and impersonality of which protect her, as if this act is part of a day's work, nothing more.

"Hello," she says, speaking loudly and rapidly when Theodore Holloman answers. "I feel so terribly awkward about bothering you—because I hear you and Bobbie are separated now—but I've been desperately trying to reach her and there's no answer at her apartment, and I wonder whether you could tell me if she's away for the summer."

She pauses for his answer, hoping he has not noticed she has neglected to mention her name. Let him simply think he is dealing with a loud and foolish person.

"Yes, she is out of town," he says pleasantly. "By the way, who is this I'm speaking to? Have we ever met?"

"No we haven't, but I'm a very old friend of hers. We went to school together. I'm sorry I never got to meet you, Ted."

"Theodore," he says, "but don't sweat it."

"You see, I've been living in Seattle all these years. I'm just passing through New York with my second husband. We're on our way to Greece. I thought it would be so wonderful to see Roberta—or rather Bobbie—again and I'm heartbroken that she's not around."

"Well, she's not very far from the city."

"Oh really?"

"I can give you her phone number, if you'd like it."

"Oh, that would be wonderful. At least I'd get to talk with her." By this time she is so comfortable in her role as Roberta's friend, she almost feels some real affection for her.

"She's sharing a house with her boyfriend and some other people—but she's thinking of staying up there with her friend on a year-round basis. In fact, she says she's determined to do it."

"How very interesting."

"I doubt Bobbie will go through with it, though. She's really a very urban person, isn't she?"

"Yes, I've always felt that way about her."

"Still, she's just unsettled enough to want to try it out. Oh, here it is," he said. "914-JK5-6213."

"I can't thank you enough," she says.

"Why don't you try calling around dinner. I think she spends afternoons at the swimming hole."

"It was really good talking to you, Ted. Lots of luck."

Shaking, she hangs up. It is probably one of the worst things she has ever done. Staring at the stolen phone number, she wonders whether she can ever use it. Is Theodore in frequent communication with Roberta? Will he ask her if she ever heard from her friend from Seattle? Will Roberta deny the existence of such a friend—and then being anyway inclined to paranoia, begin to put two and two together—particularly if Molly has called in the meantime?

On the other hand, since she has acted so far outside the bounds of normal, decent behavior, possibly no one will have the imagination to attribute such outrageousness to her. Not even Conrad, with all his talk of her vengefulness, would imagine her going to the lengths of fraud and impersonation for his phone number.

She wonders what she is becoming. She is helpless before her need to stalk him. It is as if that is her only form of connection to Conrad. She must somehow keep him alive in her own mind in order for her to continue to exist in his. *People you've been close to don't simply drop out of your consciousness, Molly.* And they *were* close, she thinks. God, they never came closer than they were at the end. They should have gone on from there—but they didn't. Her mind always sticks at that point. It is as if she must keep trying to force her logic upon the disorder of life.

"Operator, I'd like to make a person-to-person call to Conrad Schwartzberg."

There are advantages to calling long distance. The anonymous voice of the operator will protect her from certain possible confrontations. She only wishes to speak to Conrad—she has just enough courage for that.

The phone rings in his house. They have probably all finished having dinner by now, and maybe at this moment there is no one in the kitchen, which is where she thinks the phone must be located. *I would like to have a private discussion with Conrad Schwartzberg, if you don't mind.*

"Hello." A woman's voice, unidentifiable.

"I have a person-to-person call for Conrad Schwartzenberg."

"He's out in back, I think. You'll have to wait a minute." There is irritation in her voice—perhaps it is Roberta. "Who is this call from?"

The woman waits for an answer, the operator waits. Molly says nothing.

"I'm calling Conrad Schwartzenberger," the operator says.

"I'll go and get him," the woman says after a moment.

"Hello?" He sounds out of breath, a little guarded.

"Conrad—" she manages to say.

"Is this he?" the operator asks.

172

"Yes, it's he," she says.

"How are you, Molly?" he says grimly.

"Not so good. I'd like to talk to you."

"I don't know when that could be."

"Conrad—"

"Listen, what I'm going to do is write you a letter about the history of our relationship."

"I don't want a letter."

"Unfortunately, this is not a private phone. I share it with eight people. There is also someone about to come in here to try to fix the dishwasher, because there isn't one piece of equipment that works properly in this fucking house. Otherwise it's perfect."

"I'm really glad to hear it's perfect."

"I'm relaxed, Molly. I'm like a normal person. You woudn't know me."

"You don't sound so relaxed right now."

"I assure you that I am. How is Matthew?"

"I understand you're planning to rent the house for the rest of the year."

"It's a plan that has been under discussion but is very much up in the air. There are certain advantages to living out of the city as well as some real inconveniences."

"We were going to do it once. Remember, Conrad? We talked about going to Vermont."

"Molly, you remember everything. It's a little terrifying. I think you keep a catalog inside your head. Everything I've ever said to you and when and where, the precise circumstances—"

She hangs up and cries, then calls again, not bothering to get the operator this time. He picks up the phone immediately as if he had been expecting it to ring.

"Conrad, you have to deal with me! I think you really have to deal with me!"

173

"I'm doing that as best I can."

"Don't you think we have to talk about what happened?"

"I'm sure you've worked out a perfect explanation, Molly, but I have to come up with my own. All I know is that I've begun to feel in balance again—whatever that's worth."

"It's a false solution, Conrad."

"In that case, sometimes they can be the best kind."

"Oh God! You know, you really ought to hear yourself!"

"I think I mentioned the problem of the dishwasher and the lack of privacy in this situation. I'd like to ask you to try not to call again here. I'll contact you the middle of next week."

"I can't promise that, Conrad."

"Maybe you'd feel better if we made a definite appointment. I'll come in on Wednesday, August twenty-fourth, and we'll get together. I'll set aside an evening. That's seventeen days from now. I'm writing it in my book."

"Your *book*," she says.

"I'll be there at eight. You wouldn't like to tell me how you got this number, would you?"

"No," she says. "I wouldn't like to tell you."

There is suddenly the sound of rushing water, the cranking of a machine.

"Wednesday, August twenty-fourth," he says in a loud, brisk voice and hangs up.

174

I remember the Sunday night bus rides back to the city that summer, numbing the dread of returning with a fitful half-sleep from which I'd rouse myself to see if we'd gotten as far as Jersey, breathing the stale, recycled air that smelled of boredom, Matthew's head damp and heavy in my lap. I'd find a melancholy security in those times of suspension between one place and another. At least I was safe from my own expectations. Conrad would neither call nor not call. I knew he would not get on at any of the stops.

It was the Sunday before I was supposed to see Conrad that Matthew and I missed the bus we usually took and had to kill a couple of hours in town. The bus, when it finally came, was crowded with Chasidic Jews. Bearded men in dark suits and black fedoras. Women in stiff long-sleeved dresses, their hair hidden by glistening brown wigs in the beehive styles of the fifties. They carried large solemn-looking pocketbooks and pale infants wrapped in blankets.

I found a seat with Matthew in the back. Across the aisle there was room for just one more passenger. When the bus turned off the highway and made a stop at Kingston, I looked out the window and saw a small green car drive up to the terminal. A tall young woman carrying a basket got out of it. She flagged the busdriver frantically and broke into a run. It was Francine, the newest person in my office. At that time I only knew her slightly. She had never told me where she went on the weekends. I called out to her as she came striding down the aisle. She seemed the antithesis of the other passengers with her waistlength free-swinging hair, her red tie-dye shirt knotted artfully a few inches above the waistband of the cutoff jeans that showed off her long, brown perfect legs.

"This is terrific! We'll share a cab at the other end," she said as she arranged herself in the empty seat.

"Were you staying in Kingston?"

"No. Across the river with some friends, friends of my boyfriend's. He decided to stay on an extra day or so. That's why I had to come back on this. Don't you hate this ride?"

"I do it every weekend."

"Look at all these wigs," she whispered. "Can you *imagine!*" Tossing her hair, she shuddered theatrically.

"Who are you?" Matthew said.

"I'm Francine. I work in your mommy's office. I think I have a couple of chocolate cherries, if you'd like one."

"Is it a *real* cherry?"

"Why don't you try one and see? That's my dinner," she said ruefully. "They were cooking something that was going to take forever, some kind of curry thing that was probably going to be disgusting anyway. It was Bobbie's turn and she always makes a big production out of it. Unfortunately, she doesn't have any tastebuds. So I'm not missing much."

I heard the name of the person without tastebuds, I remembered the color of the car.

"What are tastebuds?" Matthew asked.

"Little buds all over the tongue."

"Do *I* have them or just special people?" A drop of wet chocolate dripped down his chin.

"Of course you have them, honey. We all do."

"Except for this one lady."

Francine sighed and then laughed. "Quite original mind you have, if you don't mind my saying so."

"I happen to know someone called Bobbie." I inserted this revelation as casually as I could. "Did you say you were staying in Saugerties?"

"No. That's *this* side of the river, I think. My friends are in Milton's Crossing. That's between Redhook and Rhinebeck. Ever go over there?"

"No," I said.

"Lots of old Dutch architecture. Rhinebeck's very pretty but awfully conservative. Milton's Crossing is just a lot of farmers and a general store. Real country, if you like that sort of thing. Of course, it's lovely in the summer. There's one couple that's thinking of staying up there through the winter—which strikes me as a little bit insane."

"Ever hear of someone called Conrad Schwartzberg?" I said after a moment.

"Of course I know Conrad. He's one of the people I was just . . . Is he a good friend of yours?"

"I know him," I said.

177

"And Bobbie . . . God, that makes me feel a little embarrassed. Sometimes it's as though I have foot-in-mouth disease."

"I can't say I know her. Years ago I met her once."

"Well . . . I don't get along with her terrifically. She's paranoid about Conrad flirting with me. If he says a word to me, she just dies. And Conrad, of course, will always come on—with me or just about any other female. If you know him, you know that's how he is."

"I'm involved with Conrad Schwartzberg," I said.

Francine fell silent. "That's heavy," she said finally. "Look—I hope I haven't caused you pain."

I looked away. "I've been in pain all summer," I said hoarsely.

"Rough," Francine said, shaking her head. "Really rough."

"I didn't even know he wasn't in Saugerties. That's how crazy the situation is."

"Extreme," she agreed. "Wow! Just think, if we didn't happen to be on this bus, it might never have come out. Now I don't know what to do exactly. Should we continue this conversation or switch to another topic? Are you a person who absolutely disapproves of gossip?"

"Not in this instance," I said.

She was a mine of information.

Our conversation wound on and on—long past Kingston and New Paltz and the string of small towns above Bear Mountain, persisting through the Sunday night traffic jams in New Jersey and the view of the Manhattan skyline above the oily marshes. The other passengers one by one turned off their lights and dozed in their angled seats. The only voices in the bus were Francine's and mine, and I wondered sometimes if any of the darkly clad

178

people heard us and what they might have made of what we said. With all their rules and their wigs, their obliviousness to the passage of time and the price they must have paid for it, they at least had the advantage of moral clarity. A person like me was an object lesson in the dangers of too much freedom.

I wounded myself with details. Conrad sleeping with Roberta on some sort of Japanese mat that you rolled up and put in a corner because she was given to insomnia and required a hard surface under her. Conrad patiently peeling potatoes and shelling peas because Roberta demanded that all domestic work be split fifty-fifty and marked all debits in red upon a chart that she hung out in public view. Conrad devoting the entire Fourth of July weekend to entertaining her family, described by Francine as "the most bougie people you would ever want to meet."

Francine had flair as a raconteur, a keen eye for the ridiculous. She was not charitable in her judgments. She condemned Roberta more on grounds of taste and style than anything really substantial. It was Roberta's "bouginess" that she objected to—more subtle than that of her family but definitely there—often taking the form of "grimness."

"Can you imagine someone skinny-dipping *grimly*? *Grimly* taking off her clothes and *grimly* going in the water. And always going on and on about the beauty of the country and getting the poisons out of your system and putting wheat germ on everything and making little references to how you sometimes have to get certain people to abandon their evil ways for their own good. That's what I mean by *grim*. I mean the utter boringness of that kind of outlook, which is simply beyond belief."

I added her version of Roberta to my own, seizing

179

upon everything negative, which was after all what I wanted to hear, because then it no longer seemed possible that Conrad could actually stay with such a person. Still what also emerged was the picture of Roberta as the one with the power, Conrad as supplicant. Perhaps that positioning was new. Perhaps it had never been the other way around, as I had thought. I wondered if her break with him had somehow caused his inability to make love to me, and if he had then gone back to her in a panic, promising her anything she wanted. He must have felt very safe with Roberta because I did not believe that he could love her. I was the evil she referred to, the reason she wanted to keep him in the country—the risk of winter isolation less than his proximity to me. Apparently she did not believe he would keep all his promises.

There is a word I detest: *interstices*. It is the name for certain very small places where one line happens to cross another, mere points on a diagram, the briefest of joinings—the lines continuing on in different directions into infinity, no final convergence indicated. As in: "I only have room for you in the interstices of my life."

It was Conrad's attempt at poetry, an effort to ennoble the situation under discussion with a tone of tragic regret. Was it his tragedy or mine? I wasn't sure. He could have said, "I'm not going to be able to see you very often," which is what I took it to mean anyway, since we had agreed already that we would see each other, but not frequently. There was a certain arrogance in the assumption that his life with Roberta would be so full he'd hardly have time in it for anything extra, just one little dot now and then.

He was going to spend it with her not in the country but in New York, in his apartment. That was what he came to tell me on the 24th, wearing a straw sombrero that Roberta had picked up in a barn sale. "How do you think this looks?" he said, preening a bit. "Awful," I said. Men like to have images of themselves in certain hats. He took it off and didn't put it on again, leaving it on the table in the hall when he took me out to dinner. He asked me if he didn't look very brown—which he was all over, as I was later to discover. I told him I thought he was looking younger, and then he wanted to know if he'd been looking old. His beard, he confessed to me, would be quite gray if he ever allowed it to grow in. I told him I'd noticed that on the days when he didn't shave.

In that disarming way he had of taking certain things for granted, he took for granted my friendship and goodwill. He was happy and therefore I would be happy for him. He couldn't help bragging a bit about his current lifestyle. His house, he informed me—as if it were truly his house, not just one he'd rented a share of until the end of September—was on a tract of one hundred acres. It had belonged to a wealthy gentleman farmer, who until his death five years before used to arrive for weekends in a private plane that would land in the meadow. He spoke of walks in the woods— *his* woods, blackberry picking and mushroom gathering, the joyous communal dinners.

"I'll bet you had curry on Sunday night."

He looked a little startled. "As a matter of fact, we did." He seemed amused by my extrasensory powers. "I'd like to keep seeing you in this casual way, Molly. I don't like to lose people altogether."

I finally let myself say what I'd been thinking. "I don't think we could possibly be casual."

182

"I know I can," he said confidently.

"Liar," I said brightly. "Liar. Liar."

"Don't you understand how wrong it would be for me to jeopardize the commitment Roberta and I have made to each other just because I cared for someone else as well?"

"Live with neither of us then."

"What? And go back and forth? Molly, I want peace. I want monogamy. I want to know that if something falls apart, it does so on its own terms."

"But we didn't fall apart, Conrad. That isn't what happened. You pulled out—we didn't fall apart. You ran, you hid."

"It amounts to the same thing."

"I can't accept that for a minute."

"I didn't hide, by the way. I retreated."

"Conrad, your house is in Milton's Crossing, not Saugerties. You and Roberta sleep on a Japanese mat because she has so much tension and she tells everybody about how she's reforming you."

He turned white. "You amaze me, Molly."

"I know a lot about your idyll."

"I never said it was an idyll. It's a rewarding and difficult relationship."

"Mostly difficult."

"That remains to be seen. I doubt that you get your information from very reliable sources."

"Only one. I'm not so powerful that I have a network."

"The person who gave you the phone number?"

"No. Actually I got that in another way."

He was staring at me bewildered, attracted, still angry. "You haven't been able to let go of me, have you?"

"Does that disturb you, Conrad?"

"It creates conflict. I think you'd actually consider sleeping with me even if I were living with someone else."

I said, "You could always refuse."

"I refuse," he said.

"Because you don't want to or because you're afraid it won't work."

"Oh it would work, but it wouldn't change anything."

We looked at each other.

"Okay," I said.

We stood up and left the restaurant. In the street outside we embraced.

"Oh Jesus Christ!" he said.

Late in September I went to see Malcolm. It was something I'd been thinking about and finally I just did it. I'd walked past his house a hundred times, looked up the stone steps through the glass door, into the little white-tiled hall with the row of mailboxes. It was odd that a person you'd once lain in the same bed with was also someone whose door you could dare to approach only in fantasy. But I had become accustomed to such apparent contradictions.

Earlier that day I had gone to Conrad's apartment for the last time. It was just before Roberta came down from the country. We'd spent the night together, our last whole night for a long while, and in the morning I walked over there with him. I had an oppressive, angry sense of *last* —the last this, the last that—unreasonable, I told myself, because it wasn't as if I were losing Conrad, it was only that certain conditions were changing for the time being.

I remember he woke me to make love just before we got up—both of us crying out with the fierce pleasure of it—and then I walked him to Seventy-eighth Street. "Do you want to come up?" he said, as if it were a morning like any other. I said I wouldn't mind. Perhaps I should have said no. Sometimes one decides to do potentially painful things as arbitrary as passing one's hand through the flame of a candle. I thought I needed concrete evidence of the change that was taking place.

She'd already begun to move her stuff in. I'd expected that. Boxes of books. And the bicycle was back. In the living room there was a maple rocker—very homey, I thought—and a large brown pitcher filled with dried ragweed and cattails, which she must have gathered in the country. There was something about the harsh shapes of the ragweed pods that I found exceptionally depressing and dead-looking, but I didn't say so. That pitcher of weeds bothered me more than anything else. It had already made a place for itself. I think I'd felt before that whatever Roberta brought into that apartment could be dismantled and taken out very quickly. Now I wasn't so sure. I tried to remember the exact way Conrad had said those words about things having to fall apart by themselves that had so encouraged me by their pessimism.

He offered to make coffee. "Will instant be all right?" he asked, filling a pot with water. He set two unfamiliar mugs upon the table and began measuring the coffee into them. They were brownish gray stoneware, very smooth, the kind that's made in Vermont. There were four more just like them up on a shelf.

I said I had to leave.

I walked around for a while and ended up in Malcolm's neighborhood. I climbed the front steps of his house, opened the glass door and entered his hall. I pressed the bell marked JANITOR. The dog began barking immediately down in the basement. I thought Malcolm would either let me in or he wouldn't. If I'd been capable of asking myself what I was doing, I might have gone away. There is a terrible risk in the exposure of need.

I remember hearing him call my name. He had opened the street door behind me.

"You didn't know I had a private entrance downstairs," he said.

I told him I happened to be passing by. "I thought I'd like to see where you live." It was a peculiar thing to be saying to someone at nine o'clock in the morning.

He squinted at me through his glasses, which slid down the bridge of his nose. He pushed them back up again with one long finger. "And why not?" he said.

It was the why-notness of Malcolm that I loved in him, his ability to act upon occasion as the moment demanded, never thinking of consequences as Conrad would have done, or measuring out the precise degree to which he would allow himself to become involved with someone *in extremis.* He was a man you could tell all your troubles to—as long as they had nothing to do with him. Guilt would tend to make him disappear, drop out of sight for considerable periods—during which he'd exhume his entire history of failure the way a dog digs up an old bone, always knowing exactly where to find it to be chewed over once again, no more nourishment in it than a mouthful of dust. Even his guilt I found attractive.

He led me down the steps past a row of trash cans and around to an iron gate. We entered a low, dimly lit passageway, pipes overhead, dusty cartons stacked against the wall. He put his hand beneath my elbow. "Watch

187

where you walk," he said. The dog Shadow was barking in a frenzy. He bounded forward upon us as Malcolm opened a door into a room whose whiteness took me by surprise. Through barred windows I could see a garden of cobblestones and ivy, ailanthus trees. The dog kept running back and forth between us, jumping up to put his paws upon our chests, panting into our faces. "Later," Malcolm said, "we'll have to take him out." I realized he was giving me the day if I wanted it.

I must have looked pretty bad, I guess. He kept talking to me in an amazingly gentle way. Would I like to sit down, even though his bed wasn't made? It was the only comfortable place to sit. Would I like scrambled eggs or just a piece of toast? Coffee? I told him he was the second person to offer me coffee and that therefore I was going to refuse. The dog climbed into my lap, front and back paws sprawling down over my legs. "He's a terrible dog," Malcolm said. "You push him away if he's bothering you." He said he was making me tea, since no one had offered me that.

I stared out at the garden, the dog breathing rhythmically against me, shedding his long red hairs upon my skirt. Finally I told Malcolm about Conrad—all of it, even about the ragweed in the brown pitcher. He said he understood obsession, that the very nature of passion was the desire to possess, which was perhaps why certain men feared to be the object of it—the fear taking different forms. His own fear—as of course he had already demonstrated—was extreme.

I have no idea what he was really feeling. I was quite conscious that I was giving him license to begin to see me now—letting him know he would be free of the burden of my desires, which were so painfully directed toward another, thus enabling us to be friends. That was even what I wanted to believe myself.

He too wanted a friend, he said.

I'm not sure he meant it anymore than I did. Perhaps, like me, he was looking to be rescued.

A sound like a dull crash five blocks to the north. BOOM, as Matthew would say, ramming his truck into a stack of building blocks. A large boom, followed perhaps by several smaller subsidiary ones. The falling apart of the house of Conrad and Roberta.

She lies very still in the mornings listening intently, never hearing what she's waiting for, although she would recognize it instantly, so well has she imagined it. Finally she gets herself up and begins to go through another day, waking Matthew before she walks into the kitchen, where if Conrad has visited her the night before, there will be two wineglasses standing in the sink. She never gets to wash them before Conrad gets her into bed. First there is the overture on the living-room couch. Then, as if taken by surprise, they rush into the bedroom, disheveled and half-unbuttoned, leaving the glasses on the coffee table. He is always careful to leave before midnight, putting on his clothes and stumbling out the door speechless with satisfied weariness. In fact, it is Molly who keeps an eye on the clock, nudging him awake at eleven forty-five. He has pointed out that it is very hard on the person you live with to be put into the position of waiting for your arrival at unpredictable hours. Surely Molly would demand the same consideration. How can his relationship with Roberta be fairly tested if he himself does not obey certain basic rules?

At any rate, after Conrad has gone and she has locked

the door, she picks up the glasses on her way back to the bedroom and carries them to the sink but cannot bring herself to turn on the water, so they are there in the morning with their dregs of wine and perhaps a dead cockroach or two drowned alcoholically—a sourness to be dealt with before orange juice and Matthew's innocent bowl of cornflakes and milk.

"What do I need to make you an egg for?" She actually rehearses herself in lines like that and sometimes succeeds in delivering them to Conrad. The egg line, for example, has a nice New York Jewish inflection, which she admires for its suggestion of hardboiled toughness, suitable to the role of a certain kind of mistress.

"Sometimes I think you only come over here to fuck." Said half-indulgently, half-seductively—although it is what she actually sometimes bitterly thinks. Would she trade that, though, for the egg? Would such a trade invariably be necessary? Ironically, it is Roberta who could shed some light on that question.

"What do you do after you leave here?" she asks him once.

"What do you mean what do I do? I go home."

"But what do you *do* ? You just get in bed with her and go to sleep?"

"Sometimes we have conversation."

"But what if she wants you to make love to her? Do you just excuse yourself?"

"Why are you asking me all these questions?"

"Is it more exciting to make love to her after you've made love to me?"

"Molly, there are nights I get into bed thankful I don't have to make love to anybody. I'm not only a political activist, I also have the small problem of making a living. I've been to Buffalo and back with some lousy dinner in an airport. Every time I make a speech, by the way, there are at least three women offering themselves—"

"That's really terrible, Conrad."

"I'm explaining to you that my life is not a picnic. You don't have any understanding of the totality of my life. You're entirely focussed on one aspect of it."

"We've spent time together, Conrad. Don't forget that!"

"I'm forgetting nothing. I'm trying to correct a very lopsided impression."

And then he reminds her that it was *her* choice, *her* choice to go on like this. He always knew how difficult it was going to be. It is hard for him too, this getting up and leaving in the middle of the night. It never feels natural. But what can he do? While Molly can tolerate the knowledge of the existence of Roberta in his life, Roberta cannot tolerate the existence of Molly. So all he can offer, until the situation resolves itself, are these truncated visits and perhaps the hope of a trip somewhere.

The trip is a completely new idea. Where and when, she demands, immediately seizing on it.

He comes up with California, perhaps because it is as far away from New York as they can go. A trip to the Bay Area in some indeterminate week, certainly before Christmas. "I'll try to sandwich it in," he says, unaware of the contradiction of speaking of sandwiches when his life is not a picnic.

We all have our own imagery. If I existed for Conrad sandwiched into the everlasting limbo of interstices, my friendship with Malcolm was an island, a warm, green place unconnected to the mainland of my life. Happiness in the middle of misery—necessary to my survival yet never quite enough to sustain me.

It was indicative of our limited relationship that Malcolm liked especially to visit me at my office. Often, having walked all the way down from the Upper West Side, he'd turn up late in the afternoon on a day he wasn't teaching at Greenhaven. The receptionist thought the whole thing was romantic. "Your young man is here," she'd say, even though Malcolm was neither young nor mine in the precise sense of that term of expression. He'd walk back with me to my cubicle, past the long row of women in the subscription department working at their gray metal desks. They'd look up at him—this erect, long-legged person in frayed jeans, bearing with him the chill of the outside. Malcolm would smile back in amused sympathy, nod to them in greeting, answer questions about the weather from which they were cut off by the absence of windows. "Is it still raining?" "Just a little." "Think it'll be over by five?" "Sure," he'd say. Sometimes one of them would flirt a bit—"Is that a promise now?" "An absolute guarantee"—laughing, the glasses slipping as they always did. A fine figure of a man. "A regular lady-killer," he once described himself ruefully.

I think he felt safer with me during those brief visits than at any other times—the bounds of possible behavior being so circumscribed. I was the prisoner in need of distraction who could be liberated only by the clock. He, on the other hand, could come and go as he pleased, thus taking the measure of his own uneasy freedom. Sitting in the visitor's chair, he'd watch me as I put the last red marks of the day upon a long proof sheet, listen gravely as I made phone calls to the printer or the author of an article. Often he'd bring with him papers from the other prison to which he had access—poems by Arnold Lewis in the same disturbing vein as the first ones he'd shown me, a newsletter also by Arnold that was to be smuggled back in and passed secretly from hand to hand. We'd stay after hours, let ourselves into the Xerox room and make illicit copies together.

"My *friend*," Malcolm used to call me, with a sadness but with a definite insistence—assuring me I was the only woman he knew with whom his relationship was not disastrous. He'd tell me about the others just so I would not be jealous. His latest disaster involved one of his most brilliant and sensitive former students, now married and studying comparative literature at Yale. She had taken the train down to New York one day for the purpose of showing Malcolm some poems by her young husband. After an hour or so of grass and intense conversation, during which she revealed to Malcolm the secret of her undergraduate passion for him—now to be safely regarded as ancient history—they ended up in his bed in the historical present, thus rounding off her education with a lesson in the inevitability of disillusionment. Her subsequent offers to leave her husband, the poet, and devote her life to her former instructor had been greeted with a silence that drove her frantic—spurring further trips to the city, letters on thin blue paper, midnight phone calls.

There was something familiar in her style. I felt a certain guilty sympathy for her desperate determination, even as I tried to relieve Malcolm's gloom. Culpability overwhelmed him. Every fresh analysis of the incident only led him back to the conclusion that he had behaved unconscionably to someone almost childlike in her openness and trust.

I told him there was no such thing as such innocence—although that was more for the purpose of argument than absolute conviction on my part. I believed in Malcolm's peculiar kind of innocence, for example—even to some extent in my own.

I railed at him in a way that he always seemed to appreciate, scolding him for what I termed his masculine presumption. "Why do you assume that everything flows from you and nothing from the other person? Do you really believe that women have no active desires—and are only acted upon by you? No wonder you can only deal with them by keeping your distance. Who could want such responsibility?"

195

I suppose there was a lot of truth in what I said. I remember he laughed painfully. "You know me very well, but not completely."

"Malcolm, I'm guessing, I'm improvising."

"Do your theories apply to what happened with us?"

"Probably. Though maybe not as much," I added quickly. "We seem to have managed to make an exception."

"Still," he said, "there's the physical distance. There's the distance between friendship and love."

I made an awkward joke at that point. "Well, if you can't go to bed with your friends, you go to bed with your enemies."

He looked at me with an ironic glint in his eyes without saying anything, sparing me the obvious question that would have had to do with Conrad.

We cultivated an honesty that never drew blood—and thus all our exhanges fell slightly short of the mark. We touched each other constantly—all within the bounds of friendship—walking Shadow for blocks with our arms around each other, lying sprawled for hours on Malcolm's bed listening to music, passing a joint ceremoniously back and forth. Toward the end, as it diminished, he would take it from between his own lips and hold it against mine. We had a comedy routine that went—

Malcolm (looking at me with mock severity): Sometimes I think that if you weren't involved with Conrad, you'd have designs on me.

Me (very warmly and reassuringly): Malcolm, you are a hopeless case of hopelessness.

(To cement this understanding they kiss, Molly deliberately pulling away before he does, Malcolm laughing.)

I reminded Conrad from time to time about the trip we were supposed to take. "What about the trip, Conrad?" I'd demand as naked he searched for his clothes in the dim light of the bedroom, the radiator chugging ineffectually as a chill blew in through an inch of open window. "What about the trip?"

I'd ask about it as if I believed it were something that would actually take place, but the question became more and more rhetorical. By the middle of November the longest stretch of time we'd been able to spend together was five and a half hours when Conrad had taken a late flight from Cleveland and phoned Roberta from my house to tell her he was stranded at the airport in a blanket of fog.

One day, though, just as if he'd thought of it for the first time, he called and said, "How would you like to go to California?"

He was going there himself for five days after Thanksgiving and thought I might find it enjoyable to be there with him—if I could arrange to leave on such short notice. He didn't exactly say he wanted me to come, but it was only logical to infer that his own desires played a part in his suggestion. Careful not to alarm him by displaying undue excitement, I said I thought I could make the necessary arrangements.

I'm embarrassed to say I felt joy. I sat in my office afterward unable to work for the rest of the day or even to think coherently at an abstract level.

Malcolm called and remarked that something good must have happened to me.

I said I supposed it was good, that anyway it made me happy.

"I can hear it in your voice."

I hesitated and then I said, "I'm going to California next week with Conrad," wishing he'd called later when some second thoughts might have begun to set in, when I might have sounded less buoyant.

"Well, don't ask me to water your plants." I think he'd meant it to be a joke, but it didn't come out that way.

"I wouldn't think of it," I said very quickly.

"Of course I will, if there's no one else."

There was a confusing silence in which I found myself waiting. Just as I would have liked Conrad to say he wanted me to come—to actually say it—I waited for Malcolm to tell me he wanted me to stay.

"You don't have to go, you know," was what he finally said.

I said it wasn't that I *had* to go—I wanted to. I went on about how much I'd always wanted to see San Francisco.

"As long as you're sure," he said.

* * *

198

BAD CONNECTIONS

In my collection of mental pictures, there is a tree I saw once from the window of a taxi, flaring up before me red and yellow just as the cab coming out of the park turned onto Fifth Avenue. In one flash I saw it through the bars of an iron fence, much too quickly to identify it. I think now that it might have been a maple. It was an anomalous tree, at any rate—the others around it being either completely brown or quite devoid of leaves of any color. It gave me a strange shock for a moment. It was all that was left of the autumn. I remember thinking that I had lost an entire season.

The taxi was carrying me to Kennedy Airport and I was alone in it. Perhaps I wouldn't have had such a thought if Conrad had been with me. I would have been preoccupied with him, with the elation of the two of us setting out on a journey. The tree, if I had noticed it at all, might have seemed a sign of something hopeful. Perhaps I would have recognized it as a fellow survivor, hanging on like me to its red and yellow.

Wasn't I making something constructive out of what might otherwise have been disappointment—his insistence that we fly out on separate planes? Roberta might offer to drive him to the airport and how could he refuse? Now that they were living together, she was apt to make a point of seeing him off and picking him up. I doubted that her reasons were entirely sentimental, but I knew the danger of dwelling upon trivialities.

My time with Conrad was to be one of reconciliation— intense conversations, lovemaking in strange bedrooms in which our rediscovered passion would reach its peak uninterrupted by the curfews that maintained Roberta's peace of mind in the East or even the awareness of Matthew stirring in his sleep on the other side of the wall.

I'd avoided the anger that could be summoned up in

199

me so easily by deciding to arrive on the Coast two days before Conrad—thus not only escaping Thanksgiving in New York, but allowing me to visit an old friend who'd been living in San Francisco and had often urged me to come and stay with her—making it plain, however, that she would prefer me to visit without Fred, whom she had warned me against marrying in the first place, and without Matthew, whose existence she approved of in theory but who would have made her acutely nervous since she wasn't used to living under the same roof with small children. Unencumbered by either, I'd known, even before I called her, that my welcome would be assured.

Women like Tessa always remind me that there are distances I will never travel. Up ahead like markers, indicators of change, they advance too quickly to be overtaken, flashing their brilliant, multicolored lights. There was always that feeling of speed about Tessa, even when we were in college, where I met her. She was always the first to do certain things—to stay out of the dorms all night on a phony pass, to lose her virginity and acquire a diaphragm, to march on a picket line and go to jail in Mississippi, to spend a summer on Bali, a winter in Tangiers, a weekend in Corsica with a French film director whom she met in Ireland when she was doing a photo essay on the IRA and who later turned out to be bisexual, although they still corresponded several times a year. She was always shedding lovers like outgrown clothes, each one reputedly more gorgeous than the last, yet ultimately lacking some vital quality; she'd try them on in different disciplines as well as languages, in varying degrees of accomplishment, of hipness, straightness, of sexual proficiency or eagerness to be instructed in the mysteries of the clitoris, the rhythms of the vagina—all to be turned loose at the slightest sign of restlessness on either part, let go without recrimination or regret. She told me once she was probably afraid of rejection, mocking herself the next moment with that generous, wide-mouthed laugh of hers in which you could see all her beautiful white teeth. We both, after all, knew she was fearless.

I was her willing audience rather than her pupil. Although I admired her style, I could no more have emulated it successfully than I could have set myself on growing taller. She liked that. She was disparaging of imitators. What I'd have borrowed from her if it had been possible was some of her ability to cut out immediately from what promised to be painful on the assumption there was always something better up ahead. I was never as optimistic. Out of an affectionate sense of duty she'd often criticize me for my tendency to get bogged down. I'm not sure she didn't prefer me that way. In the world of most of the people she knew, I must have seemed an exotic, a representative of a dying species.

She had settled into the ground floor of an old shingled and gabled house in the Mission District—an apartment decorated with tribal masks and embroidered wall hangings, beaded lampshades suitable to lovenests of the roaring twenties, Moroccan rugs, an antique black marble bathtub with gilded legs in the bathroom where she developed her photos. She took me there after she picked me up at the airport.

Sitting in the living room among the pillows of the couch on which I was to sleep, we spent some time catching up with each other. Tessa's account of her current life involved the logistics of juggling a trio of lovers, two of whom were annoyingly beginning to demand exclusivity—the journalist offering a summer in China, the stockbroker a cruise of the Pacific islands on a windjam-

mer; while the third, the one she really cared for, a paint-
er who peddled a little dope on the side, was thinking of
renting a cabin in Mendocino, moving into it with his
"old lady" and only coming down to the city once a
month. All things considered, Tessa said, it might be just
as well. She would have to think very seriously about the
trip to China; the journalist was a "beauty" in his way.
The stockbroker had his sweetness, but an extended
cruise with him might pall.

"Now tell me about this person Conrad."

I tried to do full dramatic justice to my own situation—
which in its way, I thought, was no less intricate than
hers, no less rich in its weirdness, its ironic aspects,
though there was less external action as well as a lack of
variety in location. Surely, with the right point of view,
the whole thing could be presented as an adventure.

I failed, though. The narrative kept verging too much
upon feeling and I could see Tessa growing inattentive.
She had a white cat, an enchanting slender animal that
she'd tease with a long feather, making it jump from the
floor to the bookcase to the wooden molding that went all
around the room. It would run along it with exquisite
sure-footedness before thudding down again, rather
loudly for such a small cat. "Oh, Sascha!" Tessa would
affectionately exclaim.

My voice sounded thinner and thinner in my ears as I
kept talking. I could feel the meanings I had attached to
things snapping like overstretched rubber bands. What
were these people, Conrad and Malcolm and Roberta?
What had I accomplished by leaving Fred or even now,
by coming to California? All this running after expectations anyone could have told me would come to nothing—except I always preferred finding out for myself.

* * *

202

True to form, Conrad didn't come on Friday as he was supposed to. He called from New York about an hour before I would have gone to the airport to meet him. He said he was in a phone booth on Columbus Avenue and it was freezing, and that there were some Movement friends in town for the weekend whom he absolutely had to see, and so he would be arriving late Sunday afternoon. After all, he didn't have any appointments set up until the next morning. That would still give us three days together, but maybe he could arrange to stay an extra day or so at the end.

"It's like sixty-forty!" I cried. "Remember sixty-forty, Conrad?"

"Molly, I swear to you this was unavoidable. Please don't let your feelings of bitterness ruin the little time we have to spend together."

Who could say no to such a plea?

Tessa assured me she would have shot him—"Right between the eyes, my dear, just as the fat bastard came down the ramp at the airport." I had told her that Conrad was large in response to her request for a physical description, mentioning also his blue eyes, his mass of red hair. "I've never been able to get it on with a man who had a big gut," she said reflectively. Esthetic considerations were very important to Tessa. Spending considerable effort upon the cultivation of her own body, she expected those she admitted into her bed to do the same, suggesting diets and regimens of yoga and track-running for those who fell short of her standards. "At least I always send them away in perfect condition," she'd brag. Never would she own up to the possibility that this was her way of attempting to take care of a man. Ever since I'd known her, she had quite vehemently eschewed the nurturing role of the female.

203

I remember something she said to me during one of the days I spent waiting for Conrad in her house. I realize now it was one of those statements people make from time to time in order to demonstrate that they are capable of an almost brutal frankness. Delivered more for the benefit of the speaker than the listener, they belong in the category of what Felicia once called false confessions.

In this case, Tessa thought it only fair to tell me that since she never allowed any man to hurt her, she always felt somewhat at a loss to identify with women like me, tending to feel impatience rather than sympathy—although I was not to think she couldn't be fond of someone so different from herself. Wasn't our long friendship proof of that?

I said politely that I understood.

I was very conscious of not being an amusing guest for Tessa, particularly after my stay with her was extended. I was another complication in her already complicated life—a presence on the couch perhaps inhibiting the degree of abandonment in the adjoining bedroom.

Or maybe I felt that way because I was such bad company for myself, existing in a more and more anxious state of suspension from which I could only be released by Conrad's arrival. Just as I had lost the sense of one season passing into another, I knew I would go back to New York without having truly seen California—taking with me only a blur of redwood trees and gingerbreaded houses, the first names of strangers whose faces I would instantly forget, Tessa's hand heavy with silver rings upon the steering wheel of her Volkswagen as we drove to another gathering, where I would invariably be introduced as "my old school friend from the East," as if she felt it necessary to explain me.

She had. made a date with her stockbroker for the Friday night I was originally supposed to have spent with Conrad. Considerately, but with implicit half-heartedness, she invited me to join them. He was making reservations at one of the most expensive restaurants in Sausalito, but why should he mind taking two women to dinner? Perhaps a male friend of his could be dredged up—although most of them were married and considerably duller than he was. I knew she was relieved when I told her I really felt like being alone.

I remember her elaborate preparations for the evening—every element in the *gestalt* she was constructing carefully chosen—the scent she put in her bathwater, the precise coloration of her lips, the decision not to give in to his conservatism by shaving her armpits, the silk shirt that showed the rounded outlines of her breasts, the mauve velvet jacket worn unbuttoned as a frame for the discreet bas relief of her nipples. Only her short fine blonde hair displeased her by lying too flat upon her skull. "Men like big hair," she said ruefully, squinting at herself in the mirror. She had the inspiration of wearing a purple hat at the last minute, but thought better of it. She smoked a joint and then kissed me good-bye. "You won't mind if I'm not back until tomorrow morning. It might be easier to stay at Roger's." I assured her that this was my choice and I wasn't going to feel deserted by her, however late she stayed out.

"Don't brood, Molly," she said sternly. "Fuck Conrad anyway."

"Right," I said. And then she was gone. I heard the Volkswagen start up outside.

I switched on the television and watched the news for a few minutes, the white cat staring at me, keeping her distance at the other end of the couch. I opened a can of catfood for her and emptied it into a dish. I had a sudden urge to talk to Matthew, whom I had left with my mother. I put in a call to her, but she told me he was in bed fast asleep. I'd forgotten it was ten o'clock in New York. "He's in particularly good humor," she told me proudly, "although he certainly is obstinate about taking his baths. Are you having good weather, dear?" "Lovely," I said. It would have been foolish to ask her to wake him. I said I'd call back in the morning. I'd somehow counted on speaking to him, though. "Mom!" he would have shouted.

I had an odd, empty feeling sitting there in Tessa's living room—as if I were no more than the person who had arrived on Wednesday with a suitcase and was now alone and undefined. I could not even know myself as Matthew's mother—could not go into his room to stand silently by his bed listening to him breathe, touch him as I straightened the covers. It was like the moment in the taxi when I'd looked out the window and seen the tree. *Dead,* I thought—a word which Matthew's mother would never have allowed herself to think.

The phone rang once and briefly I was Tessa's house guest. Then I turned off all the lights except one—a small lamp in the kitchen—and went to bed.

It is around four or five o'clock in the morning when the white cat wakes her. It has taken it into its head to become active, rattling the furniture in Tessa's room, scudding through papers, thudding down in Molly's dream with sounds that make her think of someone walking heavily upon a rug. She opens her eyes unwillingly upon the dense brownish light in the room—the lamp shining in from the kitchen yellowing the darkness. Now it seems that the cat must be moving around in there.

With a metallic click the lamp goes out.

"Tessa!" she calls.

Everything has become still.

Her body stiffens. She forces herself to sit up. "Tessa!"

Someone is in the kitchen treading slowly across the floor, one foot following another with deliberation. The figure of a man appears in the doorway to the living room, as if the darkness has gathered and formed itself into a shadow, as if her mind has made it take on this shape. So this is it, she thinks. And she wonders what she feels beneath the surprising calm that is like ice in her. If there is no terror, does she feel indifference? Will she die with that question?

She asks him who he is. "What are you doing here?" she says.

"Don't make any noise and you won't get hurt. You stay there and do what I tell you."

He advances upon her, stands over her—a tall, heavy-set man wearing some sort of a jacket that bunches at the waist. Black, she thinks, because of his voice and the shape of his hair; maybe a little younger than she is. She cannot see his face at all. It is too dark without the lamp. He puts his hands on her shoulders and pushes her down flat. He pulls the covers away.

She is doing what he wants. She is lying there in silence, waiting, flat out. He can see that she is obedient, but he keeps warning her, senselessly, not to make a sound.

"Don't hurt me," she says.

"Don't make a sound, don't make a sound, don't move."

Her legs are trembling because of his fear. What would he do if she were to make a sound? Would his hands close around her throat? Is there a knife hidden beneath his jacket?

"I'm very frightened." She hears her own voice, low and curiously matter-of-fact.

He pulls her legs down, dangling over the side of the couch, and bends over her. "Woman, I've been wanting you for a long time."

It is almost funny—the punch line of a ludicrously bad joke.

"That's impossible," she points out. "I only got here three days ago." He rolls her nightgown up above her waist. "You don't even know who I am," she says.

He puts his penis inside her anyway—a rather small one. There are two weak jerks and fluid runs down between her thighs. "I can't do nothin'," he says disgustedly, pulling out and wiping himself on the sheet. "You got any dope here?"

"No," she whispers.

"Don't make a sound. Don't make a sound now."

She is lying just as he left her, legs still dangling down. Standing up, zipping himself, he moves back into the darkness of Tessa's room, walking softly across the rug, disappearing through the open window into the night.

It takes her a while to realize that her belly is very cold and that her life will go on and on. On and on.

I still think of him sometimes—the premature ejaculator, climbing the back fences of the Mission District, going in and out of windows so skillfully. At least he'd gotten that much down to a science. I manage to think of him as a victim of society.

I couldn't even describe him well to the police. There isn't much you can say about a phantom. They went off anyway and got a suspect, had him standing with his hands raised up against a wall on Fair Oaks Street, drove me there with a coat over my nightgown. He was a middle-aged black man, short, thin, with a beard, a long raincoat. We looked at each other in acute humiliation. "Is that the one?" they asked. "No," I said. They nodded to him and he dropped his hands. They left him standing there without apologies.

I remember feeling that I, too, was some kind of a suspect. I didn't look much like the victim of a rape. There

wasn't a mark on me. They had me fill out a question-
naire. Age, marital status, and occupation of victim. Description of rapist and incident. What were you wearing
at the time of the rape? they asked. Was there actual pene-
tration? There was, I said. The fluid they found at the
hospital confirmed it.

The worst part of the whole thing was its nothingness.
If there is a shade of difference between something and
nothing, it was as close to being nothing as you could get.

The police brought me back that morning and I waited
for Tessa, still somewhere in Sausalito with her stockbroker. I locked all the windows, turned on all the
lights—the lamp in the kitchen going on with the same
click I'd heard before, reminding me of something I'd
learned. A fact to be kept from now on in the back of my
mind. That without your even knowing it, someone can
get into where you are.

I sat down in the kitchen and listened for footsteps, the
morning California light shining on everything, on a row
of copper pots, on Tessa's plants. The intricate shadow of
a giant coleus moved gently upon a window shade. The
cat came in and out, flicking at an empty cigarette pack
with its paw, pecking at some dry food left in its dish.

There was some stuff spilled on the floor—coffee
beans, rice. He had opened some jars looking for dope.
Perhaps that was all he'd really wanted, despite what
he'd felt obliged to say. I'd just happened to be there. Or
he could have been coming after Tessa.

I waited until it was eight A.M. New York time and
made a long distance call. Roberta answered. "I'd like to
speak to Conrad," I said.

"Oh, who is this?"

I took a breath and said, "I'd like to speak to him, if
you don't mind."

I heard her put the receiver down and she moved away

212

from the phone. I could almost see her walking back to the bedroom. She was shouting something at him. "She wouldn't give her name! She wouldn't give her name!"

"Why didn't you give your name?" he said when he got on the phone.

"Because I wanted to speak to you."

"It's her house, Molly."

"I wanted to tell you about something that happened. Someone broke in here last night and raped me."

I heard nothing at all from him. She must have been there in the same room. Finally, he said, "Are you all right?"

"I'm okay," I said. "I just feel peculiar. I'm still frightened."

"You sound all right," he said.

"Yes, I'm all right."

"Well, I'm sorry to hear such a terrible thing has happened to you," he said formally.

"Conrad," I said, "you're coming tomorrow, aren't you?"

"Yes, of course," he said in that same formal tone.

"Well, I'll see you then," I said and hung up.

Afterward I remembered that I hadn't asked him what I'd meant to—hadn't asked him to fly out right away, hadn't told him I wanted him with me. As he would have said, there hadn't been a context.

"If I'd been here when he came in, he'd have had his fucking head blown off." It is Tessa speaking. Tough talk. Her hands shake as she lights a cigarette. She leads Molly into the bedroom and opens the drawer of a small chest on the right side of her bed. There is actually a gun in it. Molly stares at it respectfully. "I'll never forgive myself," Tessa says, "for not telling you about this."

"Well, there wouldn't have been time to get it." There

could have been, though. When she'd heard him in the kitchen, she could have run into Tessa's room . . . Except that she wouldn't have, even knowing that it was there in its drawer—a present to Tessa from someone she'd met in the IRA. She always kept it by her bedside. You never could tell, Tessa said—as if rape was something you had to take into account all the time. You kept a gun in the house the way you kept aspirin.

"Anyway I couldn't have used it." It is strange to think that Tessa could possibly reproach herself for not having provided her with a weapon. There is something decidedly bizarre about this conversation. Molly feels almost on the verge of laughter.

Tessa has taken the gun out and laid it down on the bed in the middle of the satin comforter—the way you'd put down your pocketbook, Molly thinks, or lay out a change of clothes. It's like looking at one of Matthew's toys—nothing of any real interest to a grownup.

"You mustn't value yourself very much," Tessa says.

Later in the day the house is full of people—first the super and a carpenter who come to put wooden pegs on the inside frames of all the windows, then some of Tessa's friends, including the handsome but dull stockbroker. Wine and grass are passed around, and Molly is introduced as "my old school friend from the East who just got raped last night," and it is not Molly but Tessa who gives the details of the story—very agitated and highstrung, brilliantly holding the center of the stage—leading guests to the window of entry, showing just where splinters of dry wood had broken away and how the enormous rolltop desk there had been noiselessly moved aside and what Tessa would have done in Molly's place. Tessa is very sure of what she would have done, how she would have fought him off—which is what you do if you value yourself—"The guy could hardly get it on anyway. There's nothing I hate worse than *bad sex.*"

She goes into Tessa's room at one point during the party and closes the door. She sits on the edge of the bed, not wanting to lie down—even with all the people out there making it safe. Finally, she calls Malcolm.

He says a very surprising thing. "Come home immediately. I'll meet you at the airport."

Her eyes fill with tears. She is astonished.

I didn't go back to New York. Maybe it would have made some difference if I had—maybe having made his offer, Malcolm needed me to accept it. I thought the way I'd lose him would be by needing him. Whatever he gave me had to be unexpected, gratuitous—there for the moment, to be picked up or not. It was a kind of understanding that we had, a balance. It would have been disturbed by the time he got to the airport. Still I held on to what he'd said—it was like sticking your hand into an empty pocket and finding something there.

There's a loneliness in having had an extreme experience. It doesn't necessarily put you in touch with other people. Just as they step back a little, you step back into yourself—because nobody else knows the moment when the lamp went out and what you might have thought, that there might have been almost a moment of acceptance if you'd been thinking hard about your life, what it was and what it was 'not—a wavering in which you might have screamed and ended the questioning for all time. Who could understand something like that from the outside?

Tessa made me sit up all night with her after the party. We drank coffee to keep ourselves awake, the gun out on the kitchen table. She was trying to decide whether or not to move in with the stockbroker for a while, thus possibly alienating the journalist. She admitted finally to being terrified. The worst thing about rape, she kept saying, was the thought of not being in control. I didn't argue the point with her. I felt as though layers and layers of that amorphous cotton stuff they put inside quilts had been wrapped around me. In the morning I went to sleep for a while, and when I woke up that curiously insulated feeling was still with me. I reminded myself quite calmly that it was the great day of Conrad's arrival.

He came on time that Sunday afternoon, driving up in a sporty two-seater that he'd rented at the airport, quite pleased with himself for not having missed his plane— which he'd boarded of course at the last minute; or taking the wrong turn coming off the bridge; or being distracted into having drinks with two women from Stanford, who'd shared their copy of *Ramparts* with him during the flight and invited him to visit their commune. Having told the necessary lies in the East and maneuvered his way through all the pitfalls and temptations of the journey, he presented himself to me, his well-shaped lips pressing down upon mine in a kiss that was quick and ceremonial—and perhaps not entirely appropriate to the occasion, if one imagines lovers reunited after various perils enfolded in each other's arms. "See how punctual I can be," said the boy in him, grinning. Later the social worker would briefly make his appearance to ask if I needed counseling. But right now it was the boy who held sway, charmingly overgrown and scruffy, exerting the force of his radiant personality for Tessa's benefit as well as mine, wild hair springing in every direction, shirt buttons strained to the limit, hanging by threads.

"Too bad you didn't get here two days ago," Tessa said sourly.

But either way, it was bound to be anticlimactic.

I remember thinking that. I didn't feel any particular pain. There was a freedom in knowing how little I really expected from Conrad. He had come three thousand miles to be the same person he always was. It was only I who had undergone a change.

I used to be able to imagine Roberta in a very detailed way. I can't do it anymore. She's flat to me now—no more dimension to her than a cutout. I'd imagine her with hate and with an intensity that approached affection. I'd fill her out with what I knew about myself. At times she'd stand in for me, become my surrogate. She was there in the airport the night I returned from California. I had a distinct image of her waiting for Conrad in that state of resentful unease I was so well acquainted with—that condition Conrad might have called paranoia, if one can be paranoid about reality.

Until the very moment he appears at the top of the ramp, she is not even quite sure Conrad is on this plane, because she believes nothing about him very firmly. She rushes forward to claim him, throws her arms around his neck. She has a tendency to be effusive. "Did you miss me?" she says. "Yes, of course," he answers. "But I was

219

very busy." Pursing her lips, she runs the tip of one finger down the front of his coat as he begins to account for all the time spent away from her. She draws him out with little leading questions—"Meet anyone interesting?" she asks lightly, as she thinks of the phone call he got the day before he left. He spends some effort upon the description of one individual who was hostile to him for some reason, a woman named Tessa. A jetsetter, he says disparagingly. And she is relieved—he met another woman and it came to nothing while he was in California alone.

Here I wanted to intervene and give Roberta a little push for allowing herself to be satisfied so easily. I make her slip her arm through his and say, "Well, I hope you won't be getting any more of those phone calls." "That was just Molly," he says blandly, "being hysterical about something" as I walked down a ramp in a separate part of the airport.

I had flown the friendly skies of United. Conrad had come back on American. Our planes must have touched ground almost simultaneously.

I was clutching a dime in my hand, moving through a crowd of people being met by other people. There was a call I wanted to make. I think I wanted to know that someone was waiting—and then I'd be able to go home. I'd have liked just to have known—I didn't want it to be crucial.

I went and sat in a phone booth for a while. I kept thinking I was going to put the dime in, but I didn't.

It was snowing the next morning. The temperature had dropped during the night. There would be intermittent flurries for all of Thursday, according to the radio. I set out for the office in a stiff wind that blew from the Hudson, stinging my eyes with sharp little crystals that melted against my lashes. I had to keep my head down as I crossed Broadway. I saw Shadow, his rough red coat crusted over with white, before I looked up and saw Malcolm standing in front of me where the steps went down to the IRT.

"I have a friend," he said, "who takes the subway."

He was smiling at me through his glasses. I must have appeared rather dim and watery to him because his lenses were all misted over.

"It's *real* weather," I said, my intense pleasure at seeing him robbing me of more imaginative conversation. The temperature of the air was making my eyes well up.

"Unlike California. I could have told you that California does not have weather."

I said I had found that out.

He made a slight nod, looking at me very steadily. "I've been thinking about you," he said.

"I'm all right, you know. I'm getting over it."

"Not only about your condition. That isn't what I meant. Though I've thought about that as well."

"You mean the way one thinks about a friend."

"Yes," he said. "That way."

I laughed somewhat shakily. I told him I'd become very good at finishing his sentences. I stared away at Shadow who was tracking snowflakes, snapping at them as they passed. "Look at that. He's trying to eat the snow."

"That's a dog's function—to provide a source of distraction."

We were both still standing where we had been standing. The snow beat down between us. I said I was going to work and afterward I was going up to my mother's to get Matthew.

221

"Gathering your forces." He said it almost cruelly.

I could feel myself making a great effort to smile, drawing out the corners of my mouth, my cheeks aching with the cold.

"My forces," I said.

He stepped forward and pulled me against him. Two strangers couldn't have been stiffer. I put my arms around him after a while and all at once we were holding each other very tightly in our wet bulky coats. My fingers slipped into the rip just below his shoulder, pressed down beneath the sheepskin lining until I felt the warmth of the sweater he wore against his skin.

He said, "Couldn't you be late today—seeing as how you just got back from the Coast?"

Still holding on to each other, we walked to his place. He locked Shadow out in the hall. Standing in the middle of the floor, we took off our clothes, a strange solemnity in our haste, our determination to be naked.

It was like getting something back that had been lost for a long time, a quality of feeling, something profound and scary. We both lay shaking after it was over, our bodies fluttering against each other like trapped birds. I feel pain whenever I think about it, seeing it now as something that wouldn't happen again. My mind glances away from the couple on the bed. It was an ending of a sort, rather than the beginning I thought it was, shining off into the future. I even wastefully cut it short, deciding I shouldn't stay any longer. They were expecting me at the office, and it would take too much explanation if I came in later than ten-thirty. He walked me all the way to Broadway, back to the subway. "I'll call you," he said.

He didn't, of course, I spent nearly a week in a state of self-deluded happiness until I realized I hadn't heard from him.

BAD CONNECTIONS

* * *

"I have a favor I have to ask of you," Conrad Schwartz-berg says. He is sitting naked on the orange bedspread on the very edge of the mattress, having just thoughtfully removed his second sock. His left ankle is still poised over his right knee and the expression on his face is one of mingled worry and embarrassment, as if he is a small boy about to be reproached for stealing cookies. He hesitates a moment, running his fingers through his hair.

"I'd like to ask you not to bite."

Molly stares up at him.

"Please," he says. "I don't think I need to explain, do I?"

"Does she check you for marks?" Molly says unkindly. "Does she, Conrad? Well?" she says teasingly, squeezing the flesh at the base of his neck. "What if I get carried away and forget myself?"

"I'm asking you not to," Conrad says, flushing.

"Not to get carried away?" Raising herself, she puts her mouth open against his shoulder, grazes it slightly with her teeth. "The mad biter," she whispers in his ear, nipping it deliberately. "Will she think of looking there?"

"Sometimes you behave very inappropriately, Molly. I don't think I asked you anything unreasonable."

Leaning away, she makes a count of the number of moles on his back. "Did you know that you have nine moles, Conrad?"

"Thanks a lot for the information."

"I'm better acquainted with your back than you are."

She touches a spot between his shoulder blades, brings her head forward to inspect it.

"What's that?" he says.

"Just some red fingernail scratches. Not mine," she says. "I've seen them on you a lot in different places."

223

For all her teasing, she doesn't bite him again after that. Not once does she slip up. Even in the throes of the most overwhelming passion, she remembers what he asked her not to do and is therefore never overwhelmed entirely, never thoroughly lost. "Don't bite," she thinks in Conrad's voice, in that small part of herself that remains conscious, held back. The disobedience is in the remembering.

Malcolm avoided me for a while and then drifted tentatively back into my life, imposing formality upon us. He said we should agree to see each other only on certain specified nights of the week, that previously our identities had been in danger of merging—and that now we would have to be on guard against this possibility. He said nothing was more important to him than his freedom and he knew he'd have to be ruthless in protecting it— not only from me but from his own impulses. He said he felt pulled toward me in a way that disturbed him greatly, that he abhorred the institution of the family and nevertheless had fantasies of moving in with me and Matthew, that he'd actually desired to impregnate me when we'd gone to bed and that we could never again have sex without his being conscious of that desire.

I wept and felt strangely hopeful, because I knew now that he loved me. I went back to being his friend and thought of him as my lover, thought of him all the time. Even in bed sometimes with Conrad, I'd close my eyes and make a substitution; it would be Malcolm who lay upon me, Malcolm who moved inside my body. I'd will myself to think of Malcolm, quite aware of what I was doing. I'd summon him up to be interposed between Conrad and myself.

It is difficult to know what one believes in certain situations, to separate belief from desire or even the lies one tells oneself. Did I believe, as I thought I did, that somehow Malcolm and I would end up together, that at some imaginary point in the future I would have to choose between Malcolm and Conrad? I would let Conrad go, of course. How could there be any question of that? I would win Malcolm by my great patience—a quality I had not consistently demonstrated in the past. I would be patient with Malcolm because I was still involved with Conrad.

Loving Malcolm, I thought of Conrad as my sex object. He would have been horrified to have been so reduced in my thoughts, to have been dropped so ignominiously from primary to secondary place—such essential parts of his Conrad Schwartzbergness as his intellectual brilliance, unflagging energy, unfailing good humor, commitment to the liberation of women and all other oppressed groups, unfairly discounted—only his abundant fleshly self given importance. I heard him bang indignantly against the constricting walls of the little compartment in my consciousness I had stuffed him into.

In reality, men like Conrad elude such subtle forms of revenge. Their obliviousness shields them from the sticks and stones of psychological warfare. For a time Conrad was under the impression that our relationship flourished. He would often refer approvingly to my new attitude, which he found refreshingly relaxed. "How are you getting on with your friend?" he would ask magnanimously without a tinge of anxiety. It was certainly beneath him to worry about competition. Adopting the same tone, I would ask him about Roberta. He would oblige me with certain facts—she was teaching him to bake bread, she was coming down with bronchitis, she was spending three nights a week at a Marxist study group so as not to remain overpowered by Conrad intellectually.

"It's like hearing about a cousin," I said once.

JOYCE JOHNSON

"What do you mean?" he asked suspiciously.

"I mean, it's just domestic life when you come down to it. *You* have a domestic life, Conrad."

"You make it sound as though it's nothing. You don't know what a constant struggle it is to maintain it."

"Why do you struggle so hard?" I said, and then remembered that having decided the future lay elsewhere, I had begun to stop caring.

Looking for all the world like a family, they walk, deceptively, through the park, the four of them—she, Malcolm, the two boys.

He had called her that morning and said, "I'm taking my son to the park later. Isn't that what you're supposed to do with sons?" sounding strangely keyed up, incanting over the throbbing of an electric guitar, saying a walk was going to clear his head, clear his mind, because everything always looked different in the daylight, didn't it? And he wouldn't tell her what he meant, preferring to talk in riddles—something about meeting a child the evening before, "a little pale night-wandering child"—conjuring up for Molly the image of a child, someone about Matthew's size, but pale—whom he and his son Jeremy were still with, he'd informed her. "I can sense your disapproval," he said, when all she'd thought was that he was high, speaking perhaps in metaphors. He'd been upset for weeks about the visit of his son, long before the boy even arrived for the weekend. It had been almost a year since he had seen him.

It is the first Sunday in March and the lawns are brown and muddy, the trees bare, the sun surprisingly full and warm—bringing out crowds of walkers and Frisbee players. Bicyclists glide by along the paths, Conrad and Roberta-like, in pairs. Matthew gives her his coat to hold, as well as a stick he has already collected and several plastic men—because it is the function of mothers to hold things—and runs ahead to join Malcolm, this wonderful grownup who this afternoon seems entirely at his disposal. He is drunk on so much unexpected attention, a little insatiable, out of control. "Throw me the spaldeenball, Malcolm!" he yells importantly, because Malcolm has just taught him the name *Spalding*. "Throw me the spaldeenball, Conrad—I mean Malcolm!"—because he sometimes gets confused as to who is who in a given moment, seeing both men generically as not-his-father and therefore interchangeable to some extent.

Cautioned by Molly to avoid a large puddle, he glares back at her defiantly, having no patience for such dreary considerations. As he puts one foot into it, Malcolm grabs him around the waist and lifts him kicking and giggling. This sets a precedent for all other puddles that they encounter. "Now!" Matthew demands when they come to the next one, holding out his arms.

"My father really freaks out over little kids," the boy walking next to Molly says—unmistakably implying that his father is making a fool of himself. He is seventeen, fair and longboned like Malcolm, with a rather inconsequential mustache—a man almost, not very likeable so far. She has been wondering whether his air of languid sourness is something permanent. And yet for a moment now she is seized with pity for him.

"I can do without little kids myself," he says. "But I guess in your case you haven't much choice. You're stuck with him."

"Oh yes, I'm stuck," she says, making a joke of it—knowing that what he wants is the acknowledgment of some sort of alliance. For isn't Malcolm excluding her as well, even though it is her child Malcolm lifts up to ride upon his shoulders. She thinks of being touched by him as naturally as he touches Matthew, of being held without the constraint she always feels in him now, his body hardening against her like a wall; watches as Malcolm breaks from the path and runs across an empty ball field, circling it in laps, her child holding on for dear life, flushed and laughing.

"Put him down! You're spoiling him!" she cries.

The boy, Jeremy, she notices, is deliberately looking away. She remembers that he will be leaving New York on a seven o'clock train. The afternoon, by rights, should have belonged to him. She feels an obligation to do something for him, attempts to draw him out with questions about school, the concert Malcolm took him to last night—the Rolling Stones, wasn't it? She remembers Malcolm sold some books to a secondhand store to buy the tickets, but doesn't tell him that. Maybe Malcolm wouldn't want him to know.

He says the Stones are a group he *used* to like. He used to be into music more than he is right now.

"Well, what are you into now?" she says.

He shrugs. "Anything he's not into," he says finally. "Just because he's my father, it doesn't mean we're soul-mates."

She says, "I can see you're very different."

"Well, I'm not some kind of weirdo. That's a big disappointment for him to get used to."

She has an unbearable thought. Could Matthew have a conversation like this with someone someday?

"Oh, I don't know," she says. She watches Malcolm still circling the field, slowing down more and more, almost limping. She can feel the boy watching, too.

"You're out of shape, man!" He cups his hands over his mouth and yells to his father. "You're out of shape! You look terrible, man! Old man, you look terrible!" It is the first time that afternoon he has shown any animation.

Malcolm puts Matthew down and comes walking slowly toward them across the field, breathing hard, beads of sweat on his face, glasses clouded with moisture—the eyes behind them blank, unseeing.

"Tell me," the boy asks her, "what do you think of Malcolm?"

I don't think I ever assessed Malcolm, I only responded to him. I took him whole, even the troubled parts of him. He remains in my mind as someone unfinished—all the possibilities are there in him, never quite actualized.

As he walked across the grass that Sunday, for a moment I saw a displaced, desperate middle-aged man, his responses skewed, inappropriate. His shirt had come open, I remember, and as he approached my attention was drawn to the fact that around his neck he was wearing a thong with a small pointed white object dangling from it, a sort of wild animal tooth or miscellaneous piece of bone. Teenagers bought such things from sidewalk vendors in the Village. It hung incongruously among his curling gray chest hairs. I pointed at it and said, "Is that to keep evil spirits away?"

To my surprise, he gave me a very embarrassed look. And then he buttoned his shirt.

231

* * *

He turned up at my office the following day—it was like old times, when our relationship had been less self-conscious. I came out to find the receptionist chatting with him, chiding him for not coming around for a while as if he were a long lost son-in-law.

I think he had the need to tell someone about the girl in order to make her real to him—and he picked me, counting perhaps on the neutrality of the office, the gray steel desk between us, the telephone ringing into our conversation. There weren't many people Malcolm could talk to.

The piece of bone and the thong it hung on, I learned, had been a gift from the "child" he met the night he was out with his son—a female child, nineteen years old, by the name of Daria. Her wanderings, mostly disastrous, had been in pursuit of various members of rock groups, drummers in particular. Her pallor was the result of indiscriminate experimentation with too many different kinds of pills and a diet of Mallomars and No-Cal soda. I gather she was beginning to fall apart about the time she met Malcolm, looking around for an available guru. It seems to be a role that has an irresistible appeal for men in their forties.

She'd literally picked them up at the concert, he said wonderingly, both of them. There had been something about the father-son combination that had attracted her. An exquisite little waif, he called her, on her own since she was sixteen, when she'd been kicked out of a progressive boarding school in an incident involving an acid trip with one of the teachers. She had invited the two of them back to her hotel room and she and Malcolm had sat up all night on her bed talking and smoking dope, with Jeremy silent, refusing to participate. Perhaps it was shyness,

Malcolm said. He remembered being agonizingly shy at that age. Daria, with all her experience, might have seemed old to Jeremy, he thought.

He gave me an almost angry look, challenging me not to agree. I didn't think he wanted an honest opinion.

"Did Jeremy say anything?" he asked finally. "Anything about the evening?"

"Not directly. He asked me what I thought of you. It was peculiar. 'What do you think of Malcolm?' Just coolly, like that. He didn't say 'my father.'"

"He was trying to place you," Malcolm said.

"Place me?"

"Figure out who you were in relationship to me. He must have been confused because of the lack of signals. He wouldn't have asked that if he'd seen you as someone I was close to."

"Who am I in relationship to you?" I asked very quietly.

He looked distinctly unhappy. "I'm not sure," he said. "Things change. I believe in change. I have to—when the present is intolerable."

"Is that how you feel about the way things are with us?"

"The way things are with *me*," he said. "*With me.* I'm intolerable to myself. You always make me aware of that."

He stood up abruptly and said that he was going—he could see I had work to finish. I got up too. I remember I stepped forward and kissed him, much more insistently than I should have.

"You always hold on a little too long," he said.

There were various impending failures in Malcolm's life that must have made him look for a means of escape at that time. I was only one of them. Jeremy of course was another. Then there was Arnold Lewis, who had lately withdrawn from Malcolm's classes and no longer wrote poetry. He sat in his cell drawing elaborate diagrams of Greenhaven, making up what he called "battleplans." He had asked Malcolm to help him break out. I suppose Malcolm's image of himself made it impossible for him to say no. It involved bringing a gun into the prison. Malcolm could get permission to show his class a film and the gun could be smuggled in inside the projector. Malcolm said he'd have to think about it, that he'd give Arnold his answer soon—and each week Arnold would press him for a decision, his desperation more evident, his language wilder, more apocalyptic, making Malcolm go over and over every detail of the plan—until its execution and his own part in it must have begun to seem inevitable.

He must have known all the while, though, that he wouldn't do it—that he was finally not capable of going the limit, that in this he and Arnold Lewis were unalike. He used to talk about how it would all come to nothing anyway, the odds against Arnold were too great—he would be killed, or end up with an extended sentence. But sometimes he'd say that he saw how it could actually work, and then he'd speak of himself as someone whose life had lacked any significant acts.

There was never any real outcome to all of this. Malcolm never faced Arnold and told him the truth. Arnold still sits in his cell, for all I know, his plan still alive in his head—only the means of getting the gun is unsolved.

Fortune provided Malcolm with Daria. If she hadn't picked him up that night at the concert, it is possible he would shortly have found someone very much like her.

Fortune kindly dishes up the people we think we need—
not necessarily the ones we really do.

New York was just a way station for Daria—she met
Malcolm in transit, so to speak, on her way to the East in
search of spiritual enlightenment—all financed by a family trust fund. The night Jeremy left, Malcolm evidently
went back to her hotel. She moved in with him three days
later, simply turning up on his doorstep at two A.M. with
several suitcases of antique clothes, the complete works
of Castaneda, the *I-Ching, Love Without Fear* and a book
on astral projection. Eyes no doubt brimming with tears,
her small pink mouth trembling, she told him it was their
karma to be together. He was, by his own admission,
both "immensely moved" and "scared as hell." And in
that state he left with her at the beginning of April for Nepal.

As I am by nature a demander of explanations for
things that appear to make no sense, I demanded from
Malcolm before he left an explanation for why he'd chosen to cast his lot with Daria.

He said, "She is a person who is open to anything"—
meaning, I suppose, that I was not.

"Meaning that she is someone who has no center of her
own. Is that what you want, Malcolm?"

He said I was as intolerant as he'd expected. I had not
yet learned—and would never learn, in his estimation—
what it was to "go with the flow." Even now, at this inappropriate moment, when it was quite obviously too late, I
sought control. "I think you'd keep me here if you could.
You'd tie me hand and foot with your arguments."

"If I could find such arguments, I'd use them," I said
fiercely.

"Because *you* want, *you* want. I always feel you wanting and I hate it. I don't know what to do with it, Molly. I don't want to feel it anymore." He turned pale after he'd said that and pushed at his glasses. " Christ, I don't hate you," he said.

"Can you have sex with her, Malcolm? Is that it?"

Laughing bitterly, he shook his head. "I'm no different with her than I was with you."

It was Conrad's fortieth birthday in May. I bought him a ledger book bound in black with a red leather trim at the edges and a border of gold stamping. Having reached his middle years, he contemplated writing a memoir of his interesting life. I wrote with Magic Marker on the flyleaf, "A book to write your book in." I thought about signing the inscription *M.*, mysteriously, but decided finally on *Molly*. I wrote my name with deliberate boldness, making each letter as distinct as possible. It was a very conspicuous gift. I wondered what he would do with it, whether he would jettison it rather than bring it home.

He said he loved it and that it was what he had always wanted—the inscription, particularly, delighted him. He said he would certainly use it as a place to jot down his fragmentary thoughts, which he usually scribbled on little scratch pads and the backs of envelopes that got lost immediately. He said now he would surely learn to be more organized—"But probably not as organized as you." he said. Because God forbid he should abandon his endearing helplessness, which bothered me much less than it evidently bothered Roberta—who apparently nagged him all the time now because of his sloppy ways, his lateness, his habit of leaving old linty socks and underwear lying around in corners, his constant accumulation of the printed word, his tendency to wear clothes until the point of total disintegration, his interminable phone conversations during dinner and his suspicious vagueness about where he spent the evenings when she was at the study group he'd encouraged her to join.

Perhaps I was fortunate in having some of the pleasures of Conrad's company with relatively little of the housekeeping that would have been associated with it in a more conventional arrangement. Or so I told myself. I had decided that from now on I would try to want no more than I had.

I wasn't the same after my conversation with Malcolm. There is something terrifying in finding that someone you thought you knew well has all the while been concealing a profound resentment of you, almost a revulsion. I've known that feeling myself with perfectly acceptable men who've pursued me too hard when I did not want them—I've found myself cornered and gagging, gasping for breath. Did I suck the air from Malcolm's lungs at the very moment I thought I was being patient? Did some fatal essence emanate from me at all times, striking terror into the hearts of men—what Malcolm called wanting, what Conrad called pressure? And yet the want was innocent, I'd thought, entirely well-intentioned. What did I want but love? Where was the loss to them in that?

* * *

"Have you noticed," Conrad said, "that our sex life has become extraordinary?" Rolling off me, he made a grab at the pillows and stuffing three of them under his head, propped himself up for a brief session of analysis of this phenomenon. "Theoretically, at least, we should be experiencing a decline at this point. How long has it been—two years?"

"Theoretically," I said, "with less psychological involvement, one can concentrate more on the act."

A look of worry momentarily came over him. "You say the damnedest things, Molly."

"I'm saying," I said thoughtfully, "that perhaps I finally understand you."

"And what do you understand?" he said, smiling indulgently.

"That you are the way you are."

"You've given up on me then." The smile still held. "Bitterness has led you to underestimate me."

"Conrad, you should be going home. It's getting late."

"I feel you underestimate me, Molly—and it's certainly not pleasant. You've written me off in a way, formed certain judgments."

"I've only come to accept the situation. Isn't that what you've wanted?"

"Molly, I know you." He laughed in disbelief.

"Not entirely."

"Bullshit. I know you inside out. Especially there." He put his hand between my legs.

"I know you there, too."

"So what's all this about lack of involvement?" he said hoarsely. "Whose lack are talking about?"

"Maybe mine," I said.

239

"A new twist, Molly. Two years of guerilla tactics—but you've never lied. What do you hear from your friend Malcolm, by the way?"

"I don't hear anything."

"Have you written him off as another hopeless case? But maybe you're only attracted to lost causes. Look at Fred, for example. And then of course there's me. What do you think that means, Molly? What would become of you if you ever won?"

I didn't answer that question—it would have led me over a mined terrain. Conrad was always a better tactician than I was.

I used to tell myself I'd definitely go to the grave alone, and that this was the time to start gettng used to it.

I'd look in the mirror over the bathroom sink each morning to see if overnight I'd gotten older, tracing each new faint line upon the skin, finding a hair that had grayed and coarsened, become peculiarly tenacious. I could read my fortune in these signs.

I was not yet alone, of course. It was only a rehearsal. In case, I thought.

Roberta took a lover that spring—someone in her study group—took him officially by Memorial Day weekend, when they went off to Provincetown together. He was twenty-two years old, a graduate student in philosophy who sold Sabrett's hot dogs in front of the Forty-second Street branch of the Public Library. Previously he had often dropped over to ask Conrad's advice on how to organize the hot dog vendors of New York, a project he and Roberta were working on jointly. This serious young man saw the hot dog vendors—supplying, as they did, lunch for large segments of the working class, although members of the middle class as well were known to be tempted by the steaming franks in the cold buns soggy with onions in chili sauce—as a potential revolutionary force of great value.

"Sincere but naive," Conrad sighed to me, shaking his head. He theorized that Roberta had reached a stage in her development where she needed someone she could dominate.

We spent the weekend Roberta was in Provincetown together, Conrad considerately returning to the apartment on Sunday night so that she would not come home to an empty huse. It was important, he said, for Roberta to validate her independence and selfhood without being punished for taking such a vital step. He proudly pointed out the contrast between his attitude and that of my ex-husband's.

"I have never felt that I possessed Roberta," he said. "That would be a contradiction of all my principles."

Despite the rhetoric, his tone was melancholy. He confessed to a slight feeling of displacement—which of course was to be expected.

Being an expert in hurt feelings, I pointed out to him that his feelings were hurt.

"How little you understand me," he said.

And yet it got to him.

By the middle of the summer, Roberta's affair was still going on. She would come home after spending a day or two with her Sabrett man and she and Conrad would have endless discussions, separating her positive motives from her negative ones—which had to do with her accumulated hostility toward Conrad and her desire to compete with him. They were finally having what Conrad called "a very open relationship."

I remember him saying at one point that he was lonely.

241

To live with someone preoccupied entirely with herself was a very lonely thing, he said.

My first reaction was not sympathy. Conrad was not entitled to sit in my house and speak to me of his loneliness—me, of all people. In fact, such self-indulgence enraged me.

"Conrad, you arrange your whole life so that you're never alone," I pointed out. "You have at least two girlfriends, eighteen meetings a week, fifty million other people whose liberation movements you've promised to organize personally. And your big complaint is always that you don't have solitude. Maybe you're lonely for two minutes when you're in the john—but that's about it, Conrad. I'm not about to discuss it as a major problem."

Head bowed during this tirade, Conrad pulled at clumps of his curls. When I was finished, he looked up at me reproachfully. "You never think of my life as painful."

"Painful, perhaps. But not lonely."

"Because I have *at least two girlfriends*," he said in an injured tone.

"I wonder sometimes if there are others."

"No, Molly. There are not." He spoke with weariness and sadness.

"Well, only two then," I said more gently.

"Molly, I can appreciate how hard it would be right now without you." His blue eyes were slightly filmed and bloodshot, yet intense.

"Well, maybe I should let it be hard, Conrad," I said. "Maybe I should remove myself and let it be hard for you. Maybe you'd learn something from that. Except you'd probably just find a replacement."

"You couldn't be so easily replaced. I need you, Molly," he said with feeling. "Even Roberta knows that—on some unconscious level. I could tell her I was seeing any other woman in New York, but you're the one she has the obsession about. She says that even though she knows you've gone from my life, she feels you cast a shadow over our entire relationship."

"But I'm not gone from your life," I said.

"That's beside the point. The shadow's certainly there."

"But I don't want to be a shadow. I hate being a shadow."

"Maybe someday you won't be," he said too quickly.

"Don't ever say things like that to me unless you mean them."

"I mean them, Molly," he said.

I acknowledge Roberta's contribution to my psyche. The concept of shadow, of shadowhood. It was a clarification of precisely what troubled me and of what I wanted most from Conrad or any man—the permission to be real. To be neither a shadow nor a category of experience, but myself—whatever that was. I had thought it was the other way around—that Roberta shadowed me; that because of this, it was I who was obsessed with her. Now I saw us both as incomplete—dark, two-dimensional figures wafting diaphanously through Conrad's imagination like restless ghosts. He denied both of us existence. Therefore he was lonely. I don't know why, but I always felt closest to Conrad when I was sorriest for him.

In late August a postcard arrives.

The swirling wake. Ship's lights upon dark waters. Flying fish glide between troughs, scatter phosphorescence at lift-off. The wind indolent but unamused. Occasionally seasick but blissful.

Malcolm

It is dated May 22, written aboard the freighter *Samuel B. Paterson*, mailed from Calcutta. There is of course no return address.

For a few days she ponders the word *blissful*. Can one be blissful and seasick at the same time? If so, that is bliss indeed. Troubled, she walks in the park deliberately past the hill where the cherry trees, blossomless, are in full leaf. Green trees like any others.

* * *

Conrad went to California the way Malcolm went to India. It seemed a solution. The state of California gets a lot of its population that way. You can always go there when you don't know what else to do with your life.

Someone called Conrad in September and asked if he wanted to work on a case in San Diego—three Chicano farmworkers were accused of shooting a state trooper who'd attempted to break up a demonstration. He made up his mind in one phone call. He flew out there over a weekend, met with members of the defense committee, and took a three-month lease on a garden apartment with a swimming pool, which he described in glowing terms on his return. Why shouldn't he have a swimming pool? he said a bit defensively. Even the workers had swimming pools in California. He said mostly he wanted to have a separation from Roberta. And from me? I asked. Of course not, he assured me. He was finally going to do what I'd often suggested—take time to think, to sort out his relationships. He was going to devote special thought to the one he had with me.

I understand from what Francine told me later, long after the fact, that he asked Roberta to come out with him. She is quoted as saying she had too many irons in the fire. I understand he proposed marriage and that she said it was an outmoded social form, which of course he would have had to agree with.

Next or before or simultaneously, he asked me to make a trip out there to visit him—ten days in October, after he'd gotten himself situated. It was going to be very different from the last trip, he assured me. We were going to take a drive all along the coast. And since we'd be only fifteen miles from Mexico, he'd take me there for a weekend. We'd bathe in the Pacific and review the history of our relationship. He got quite enthusiastic about the idea. It was our chance, he said, to come to some decision about the future.

I thought of it as one last try.

Conrad addressed a rally of thirty hot dog vendors the day before he left.

When I was five, I had a romantic attachment to a boy of seven who tormented me by threatening me with snakes and witches. He went away to camp for the summer and promised to bring back a bear who would devour me. He said he would keep it in his garage—a logical place. I didn't tell my mother, not wishing to upset her. For two months I counted off the days of my life. I looked out my window one day and saw that my friend was back. He was bouncing a ball against the fence in his back yard. The garage door was shut. I thought I would go down there and confront my inevitable fate. I counted off my final hour.

"What about the bear?" I said, walking right up to my friend, not wishing to waste any more time.

"What bear?" he said, puzzled.

I wept in fury because he had forgotten something that was so important to me.

Was that the beginning of it all?

Molly, you always hold on a little too long.

I have always been too faithful to the illusions of others.

Love.

We took a trip that Sunday in California, leaving San Diego early in the morning and heading south toward the border. Conrad was going to show me Mexico for a day. True, originally he'd said we were going to spend the weekend there. But a day was what it came to. Still he thought we could get all the way to Ensenada and back— not that that was the *real* Mexico; we would have had to go much further for that.

We crossed the border into Tijuana, leaving California behind in the diner where we'd had breakfast, squeezing lurid blue syrup out of plastic containers onto pancakes that were all too pink—a veritable sunset in the plate. A different, foreign shoddiness awaited us. A swarm of peddlers and skinny children invaded the slow-moving traffic, running along beside the cars offering false pottery, bulbous glazed pigs, planters stickily varnished

painted with cacti and sombreros, religious figures hide-
ously gilded—the sun glistening pitilessly on everything,
the broken streets, the bruised facades of houses, the raw
dirt hills with never a tree in sight, just the shanties, one
piled on top of another. "You're looking at the Third
World," Conrad said, taking the back streets deliberately
just so I could see it before we got on the highway that
led to the sea.

I stared out the window with dismay—and yet with an
unfamiliar happiness, because he, Conrad, was showing
me this misery he'd seen a hundred times before and was
probably even bored with because of its very hopelessness. No question that he was doing it just for me—the
car bumping over the deep ruts, the stones and shards of
bottles, the flattened-out cans; the heat-baked dust rising,
settling on the windshield, sifting in upon us. Yes, I was
happy, grateful, even distinctly optimistic, sensing
change around every corner—like the promise of an icy
bottle of soda pulled wet out of a freezer. Coca-Cola,
Orange Crush, any flavor would have done. In the window of a little shop, I spotted a dusty Pepsi sign. "Let's
just keep going," Conrad said, "We'll get some later." He
seem possessed by the desire to drive without stopping. I
would have liked to have gone into the little shop.

We took the coastal highway, the blue Pacific glinting
at us between cliffs and behind *Turista* signs advertising
shabby motels and shops selling more damn pottery—
enough planters for every patio in California. He said we
would find a beach somewhere, but it always seemed
hard to get down to the sea. You'd end up in a parking lot
with the blue water three hundred feet below. Still, it was
sort of beautiful. We went inland for a time, winding
though little mountainous roads hardly ever passing a
person or a house, just a few cattle in a dry field sometimes. And once in the middle of nowhere there was a

huge sign plowed into the side of a hill, JUAN LUIS POR-
TILLO. I am remembering all these oddments very clearly. The fact that we never once stopped that day to have a
drink and I was thirsty and wouldn't say it. As if only he
could decide to stop, not I.

We found a beach in the late afternoon—not a beach
exactly, but another parking lot by the side of the road
with fine black gravel underfoot. You could get very close
to the water, though. There were rocks you could climb
down and sit on. He went ahead of me down the cliff and
I scrambled after him rather cautiously because I am not
much of a climber. We each found a rock. We sat facing
each other looking out to the sea. He had for some reason
brought a book, but he didn't read it. We'd look at each
other sometimes. I don't think we said much.

A Mexican family drove up into the lot above us and
got out of their car. A middle-class family, an older man
and woman and a young couple—the women stiffly, incongruously dressed in pants suits. Standing on the gravel, their backs to the sea, they all took pictures of each
other for a while, then got in their car again and drove
away.

We sat a while longer, maybe twenty minutes. It was,
for me, the best time we ever spent together. I think I was
perfectly happy. I'm not sure why exactly. Maybe because of the stillness, maybe because we could finally,
for once, just sit with each other like that, not even having to say anything, and yet have it complete. We'd had to
cross a border to be that way with each other. It was
something much rarer than passion, much harder to get
to. I think—I am sure—he felt it too.

I didn't want it to end. I with a child waiting back
home in the East and a living to earn—a responsible person, I would have gone on with him if he'd asked me, disappeared with him into Mexico, moving farther and far-

ther South, all his commitments and mine forgotten. I was ready to take any risk, any leap—my mind crazily seizing out of thin air practical solutions to what in sanity would have seemed impossible. *I'll call my mother and ask her to keep Matthew for a while. I'll ask for a leave of absence from my job.* I computed the balance in my checking account. I saw myself breaking free of everything that bound me.

"It's getting late," he said. "Let's take off for Ensenada so that we can drive back before dark."

Ensenada was as far as we went. It wasn't much of a town. No charm in particular. The houses on the dirt streets were slightly better than the ones in Tijuana and the same pottery was for sale. I could have lived without seeing Ensenada. We drove through it, then turned around and drove out again. He showed me a *cantina* where he had once had drinks—with a friend, he said. He said it was a terrific place, but we didn't stop there.

There was fog on the road up the coast, billowing veils of it rolling in from the sea. I looked out the window for the beach where we had been, but somehow I missed it. He was driving rather tensely, his eyes straight ahead on the road. I told myself I was still having a good time.

Just outside Tijuana there was a sunset. Ah, the purples, the golds, the fiery rose in the center of it, the mysterious shafts of light piercing through clouds straight down to the sea, the warm shadows on the cliffs. Who can deal with a sunset like that? It is the kind that makes banal postcards or paintings that are a humiliation to the artist. It is as if the human eye flinches away from such beauty, is somehow unequal to the viewing. It is the same way with happiness, perhaps. Once one identifies it, grasps after it, it has already come and gone.

He is in the kitchen of the garden apartment with the swimming pool catching up on his calls. In the next room Molly, having washed off the dust of Mexico in the shower, is lying on their bed.

She thinks of it as *their* bed only by virtue of the fact that she will be in it with him for a few more days, then it will become *his* again. There are exactly four and a half days left. The rest of the room is clearly his, dominated by his scattered possessions—articles of clothing she realizes she does not recognize, electric razor, tape deck, typewriter, a pile of paperbacks and unanswered mail on top of the desk. Also the ledger book she gave him for his birthday—"A book to write your book in." How odd to see it there. But it pleases her that he has brought it with him. She wonders if her inscription is still in it, although there is no reason to think it should not be.

She has opened the copy of *Middlemarch* she brought with her from the East. She can hear Conrad's voice very plainly. First he talks to several members of the defense committee, then to a student at the university who is evidently inviting him to be a speaker at a teach-in. That is only a short conversation. He hangs up and walks into the bedroom, smiles approvingly at Molly. "Reading?" he says. He puts a cassette on the tape deck and turns it on. A Mozart serenade for woodwinds. He stands listening to the opening passage by the flute, then walks out of the room again.

The oboe picks up the theme, plays a slower, slightly mournful variation. In the next room the phone is being dialed. Now Molly lies very still on the bed, hardly daring to move—her sense of hearing suddenly sharply attuned like a fine precision instrument to pick up both levels of sound, separating one from the other—his voice under the liquid, innocent stream of notes. She cannot quite hear what he is saying, but there is a drop in the tone into intimacy. A few words are distinct—"No, no, I got your letters . . . " A little while later he says quite loudly, "I'm not speaking in a low voice. I happen to have a frog in my throat." As if in demonstration, he coughs three times.

She cannot look at him when he comes back in. She pretends to read, her fingers clenching the book, her mouth stretched tight over her teeth. He does not sit next to her on the bed, but goes to his desk and pulls open drawers, rummaging through papers. She does not think she is going to cry. This is a new, much colder feeling that she has now—the severe implacability of a judge. Not for the world would she even explain to him what it is that is so wrong. *So we could not even have one day.* No, she will never say it. She turns an unread page of *Middlemarch.*

The Mozart ends. He selects another tape, a Brahms

quartet. He walks over to the bed and sits down now, a piece of folded paper in his hand with something inside it.

"You know what this is?" he says.

"No." She scarcely looks up from the closely printed lines of type.

"Hash. One of the students I met here gave it to me."

She is silent.

"I thought we'd smoke it," he says.

"I've never had it."

"Wouldn't you like to try it out?" He gets up again and goes back to the desk, looks for something.

"I'll try it out," she says.

Now that he has made this suggestion, she knows that what she would like to do most at this moment is get out of herself in the most literal sense of the term. She would like to climb out of Molly, the reality of Molly and Conrad. Finally, she thinks, she understands addiction.

He comes back with a small glass pipe. "This was also a gift," he says, holding it up, delighted with his new plaything.

"Oh, people really like you, Conrad. They like you a lot. I'll bet that was from a woman, wasn't it?"

He seems confused by her tone, almost hurt. "I don't care for what you're thinking."

"But you don't *know* what I'm thinking," she says, the bantering note still in her voice. She feels brittle—brittle as the pipe which might snap in your fingers if you put too much pressure on the glass. *So we couldn't even have one day.* Even if she did say it, he wouldn't understand. And Roberta the one being lied to on the phone this time, long distance. No pleasure in such reversals. A Pyrrhic victory. She savors the word *Pyrrhic*—the taste of acid in it.

Later, when they are both sufficiently high, she asks, "Did the frog go away?"

"What frog?"

"The one in your throat."

"You crazy little cunt," he says.

"Is that what I am?"

"Yes. Crazy."

They have been lying next to each other without touching. Now in an abrupt, purposeful way, he rolls over on his side and pulls open her robe. "I'll put a frog in you," he says. "I'm going to fuck you like you've never been fucked before."

"Oh, I've been fucked that way many times." It is she who is speaking over long distance now.

"But only by me."

"Oh, yes. Only by you."

She watches him come down upon the woman's body on the bed. She lies unresistant, removed, his open mouth moving, sucking, the tongue playing insistently on the nipples, the hard fingers going inside her and then the mouth there too. She hears herself moan and the mouth bites, consumes. She struggles against it.

"Don't you like me to hurt you? Don't you like it?" He holds her down, laughing. "You do, don't you?"—thrusting himself up, his lips on her mouth, her own taste on them.

Behind her closed eyes, there is a picture flashing in her brain, a picture of a woman holding a monster of corroding flesh in her arms, white, pulpy corroding flesh engulfing hers as she pulls him into her, embracing him, opening her legs. The monster rides her now, urging her on, curbing her, demanding and taking more.

"Does it feel big?"

"Yes," she whispers.

"This is what you want."

"Further," she says. "Further."

"Like *this*?"

"Oh!" she cries.

"Your cunt is so open. You know that?"

She holds the monster in her, rocks him, encircles him with her soft walls, until her flesh glows like a coal and he bursts inside her transformed into a shower of light.

The last words Conrad Schwartzberg ever said to me are not particularly significant.

"Take advantage of the pool."

He was on his way to a meeting. Something to do with the defense committee, I believe. Or was it the student group. He was going to be back in time for dinner.

I was alone and so I looked in the ledger book still on top of the desk. I wasn't intending to read it—just see the flyleaf where I had written my name.

It had been half torn out very sloppily. You could see the jagged edge along the binding where the top part of the page had been. Only the bottom part, which was blank, remained.

What I remember most clearly about the next few hours is the taxi ride to the airport—the feeling of speed, of having jumped off into space. I rolled down both windows in the back and let the hot dry air blow in upon me. I was walking out, I thought, over three thousand miles.

On the plane I began to feel strange. I kept thinking I'd forgotten something—although I was sure I'd packed everything I'd brought with me. Finally, somewhere over the Rockies, I remembered I hadn't left a note.

Every now and then for a while afterward I had an urge to call him. It was like having committed suicide and knowing, that if you wanted to, you could find out what someone had to say about it.

I never spoke to Conrad again—although one day I phoned Roberta.

I said, "I think it's only right to tell you that I was recently in California and it's all over now between Conrad and me."

"Why are you telling me this?" she said.

I said, "I really think we have a lot to talk about. I'd like to get together with you and have coffee."

I actually had a vision of some great communication taking place between us, after which everything would be finally understood.

She said in a rather strangled voice, "I'll call you if I think it's a good idea," and hung up.

I am living what could be termed an orderly life. Sometimes in the mornings if I wake up very early and am by myself, I have disquieting thoughts. They begin to pass when I get up to make breakfast. I drown them in frozen orange juice, in the rush of water into the sink that washes away yesterday's coffee grounds. I wake Matthew and get him ready for school. Since there is no one here to object, I let him turn on the Flintstones as loud as he wishes. I worry sometimes about the effect of so much mass culture upon his consciousness—yet he seems to be surviving the onslaught, to remain very much himself, joyous and critical, imaginative. He spends Sundays with Fred with some regularity, even sleeps over. Fred has been seeing a woman steadily for a while, but Matthew, loyally, never mentions her. I miss him when he is gone, although I am glad to have a night to myself. There is a stillness in the house that does not altogether please me—like the moment every morning when I return to the apartment after I have put him on the bus to school. I know that I am walking into an empty place. I finish putting on my makeup, feed the cats, have a last cup of coffee and go to work. There is something to be said for routine.

I have dieted and lost ten pounds. My friends tell me I have never looked better. In two years I will be forty. I wonder what it would be like to look my age. Or act my age. I would like a life uncomplicated by longings.

I sometimes think that Conrad Schwartzberg was my last great passion. The thought invariably brings tears to my eyes. And yet it is clearly better to live without such disruption. If I have lost the hope of ever being completely happy, I hope I have also lost a certain vulnerability to disappointment. I try to be more cautious now. I always believed in being led by emotion, but perhaps I am beginning to change.

Roberta never called back. For about two weeks I thought that she would and then I knew she wouldn't. She and Conrad are still together, although I understand he spends several months of the year in California, where it is rumored that he has a new girlfriend, a very young one this time. Perhaps geography makes the situation bearable.

Malcolm occasionally sends a postcard from some exotic part of the world. I give the stamps to Matthew.

I find that with my mind less occupied with thoughts of either Malcolm or Conrad, there is a lot of room in it for other kinds of reflection. Felicia has been urging me to go back to school to get my Ph.D. Lately I have become interested in Latin American literature.

In some ways I have never been more productive.